A MIGHTY
FORTRESS

OTHER TITLES BY FAITH BLUM

Hymns of the West Series

A Mighty Fortress
Be Thou My Vision
Amazing Grace
Lily of the Valley
The Solid Rock

Hymns of the West Novellas

I Love Thee
Pass Me Not
Redeemed
Life and Salvation
Just a Closer Walk
Just As I Am
Blessed Assurance

Short Stories

Where the Light May Lead
Heaven's Jubilee and Other Short Stories
Faith is the Victory

A MIGHTY FORTRESS

Faith Blum

Paperback Second Edition
September 2016

ISBN-13: 978-1537540146
ISBN-10: 1537540149

Cover by Perry Elisabeth Design
        perryelisabethdesign.blogspot.com
Road image courtesy of imma
        morguefile.com
Layout: Penoaks Publishing
        penoaks.com
Editing: Kelsey Bryant
        kelseybryantauthor.weebly.com/editing.html

For my friend, Garry,

who was a constant encouragement to me

throughout the entire writing and editing process.

TABLE OF CONTENTS

AUTHOR'S NOTE

In Jed Stuart's part of the story, I use the term "Da" to refer to his father. This is intentional. Iain Stuart is Scottish and "Da" is the term many Scots use when referring to their fathers.

Also, for those of you who live, or have lived, in Wyoming and Montana, I realize that some of the terrain may not be completely accurate. I tried to keep it as close as possible, but sometimes characters simply take over the story you are writing about them and do things that you least expect, or the story will dictate what needs to be done. Thus, either I or my characters may have manipulated some of the terrain in the story.

He that dwelleth in the secret place of the most High
shall abide under the shadow of the Almighty.
I will say of the Lord,
He is my refuge and my fortress:
my God; in him will I trust.

Psalm 91:1-2

The Lord is my rock, and my fortress, and my deliverer;
my God, my strength, in whom I will trust;
my buckler, and the horn of my salvation,
and my high tower.
I will call upon the Lord, who is worthy to be praised:
so shall I be saved from mine enemies.

Psalm 18:2-3

Be thou my strong habitation,
whereunto I may continually resort:
thou hast given commandment to save me;
for thou art my rock and my fortress.
Deliver me, O my God, out of the hand of the wicked,
out of the hand of the unrighteous and cruel man.

Psalm 71:3-4

CHAPTER ONE

Robert ran out the back door of the house and into the barn. "Daddy, Uncle Joshua! There's a letter from Grandpa and Grandma!" He stood in the doorway and pointed toward the house. "Mommy said it's probably about their ranch."

Joshua exchanged a glance with his older brother, Matthew. *Could it really be true? Have Pa and Ma finally found their ranch?* His parents had left him and his younger sister, Ruth, in Matthew's care while they went West to find a ranch in the Wyoming or Montana Territories.

Joshua's brown eyes danced as he jogged a few steps toward the house. He looked back toward the field and noticed that Matthew followed at a slower, almost reluctant, pace. Joshua came to an abrupt halt halfway between the barn and the house as he realized that Matthew had been resistant to their parents' plan to move West ever since his pa had mentioned his dream of owning a horse or cattle ranch. Matthew loved having all his family around him. He had grown up with three sisters and one brother and had always been around his family, even after he had married Leslie. Even now, two of their sisters were married but still lived nearby, and Matthew visited with them often. Joshua decided to tamp down his excitement so he wouldn't rile Matthew too much. At least he would try.

Unlike Matthew, Joshua had been in complete agreement with his pa. Going out West had always been a dream of Joshua's almost as much as his pa's. Joshua's feet nearly jumped onto the porch steps as he hurried into the house. He glanced back again for a quick look at Matthew and noticed that Matthew was still following, very slowly.

Joshua rushed through the door and saw his nephew and niece hovering excitedly around their mother. With a quick glance he noticed Ruth quietly scrubbing the rest of the flour off the table, her brown hair still neatly in a bun. The smell of fresh bread dough still hung in the air, tempting Joshua's already empty stomach.

Matthew's wife, Leslie, looked up as Matthew walked through the door, his wide shoulders brushing the edges of the doorframe. She smiled as he nodded at her to read the letter.

Leslie's voice was sweet and clear as she read.

August 15, 1875

Dear Family,

It is with great joy that we write to you. We found a ranch! This is a dream come true for both of us. The ranch is just outside Cartersville, Montana, and will be perfect. We can't tell you how wonderful the ranch is. You must come out here to see it for yourselves! But, since we know many of you will not be able to, we will do our best to describe it.

When you ride onto the property, the first thing you see is the hills. This land is definitely not flat! The hills are everywhere. The land has some flat areas, but certainly not very many. The property has a small cabin to the left and a few run-down fences. The cabin will do until Joshua and I can build a house. We already have the perfect spot picked out for our new house. It is off the "road" aways and on top of a hill overlooking the mountains to the west.

Oh, the views from some of these hills! Ruth, you will love wandering the property reveling in God's beautiful creation. We expect a few poems from you. The mountains are a hazy blue all the time. The sight of them takes your breath away. I cannot imagine what they will look like in the winter. Even from this distance we can see the snow on the tops of the mountains.

At night, the stars are phenomenal! You can see so many of them. It is truly amazing that God would give us so many blessings. All that is missing are our two youngest children.

Enclosed you will find money for the stagecoach for Ruth and Joshua. We hope to see you as soon as Matthew can spare you.

Love you all,
Pa and Ma

Joshua was the first to speak. His voice was tinged with excitement. "Can I go to the stagecoach office and get the tickets?"

"Pa didn't say anything about wanting you two out there yet."

Joshua felt as if his jaw would drop to the floor. Looking around the room, he saw Ruth's raised eyebrows, Leslie's narrowed eyes, and Robert and Eliza both looking between the older people.

Silence reigned for a full, horrible minute while Joshua fumed. His quick temper exploded. "So?" he asked. He would not have been surprised if flames had shot out of his mouth. "What did he have to do? Say, 'Make sure you send Ruth and Joshua with the next letter'?"

Matthew scoffed and looked away. "No, but he didn't say you were to go yet. He said 'as soon as Matthew can spare you.'"

"He sent the money for the travel expenses." Joshua's voice rose to the rafters as he failed to rein his anger in. "How much more obvious can you get?"

Matthew's eyes narrowed. "I still need your help getting the wheat in. After the wheat is in, then we'll discuss it."

"After the wheat is in?" Joshua was incredulous. His eyes met the wide, frightened brown eyes of his niece and he forced his voice lower. "After the wheat's in, you'll say we need to wait until after winter. Then it'll be planting time and you will never let us go. We'll be forced to be your slaves forever! Matthew, you wanted this farm. You did fine without us before Pa and Ma left us here. You can do it again." His eyes narrowed as he hissed, "Pa and Ma need us more than you do."

Matthew gritted his teeth and glared at Joshua. "That is enough, young man!" His voice was tight and forced.

7

Joshua walked around the table, hands balled into fists, and stood right in front of Matthew. "Anytime you want to fight this out man to man, let me know!" He stormed out of the house, slamming the door behind him.

Matthew's eyes bored holes through the door. He did not even look at anyone else as he followed Joshua out the door.

Joshua and Matthew worked side by side the rest of the day, speaking to each other only when words were needed. Ever since they were kids, they had often clashed because they were stubborn, bull-headed, and harbored their anger until something, or someone, broke through to them.

For three days, the tension was high. The two men refused to speak to each other unless absolutely necessary, and everybody was miserable.

Saturday night, Matthew announced that they would not be going to church the next day. "The weather will be good and we need to get the wheat in before it rains." He ignored the condemning look he received from his wife and sister. Joshua was too exhausted to respond.

As Joshua went to bed, he heard Ruth and Leslie whispering suspiciously together. He shook his head. "Girls," he muttered under his breath and dragged himself into bed.

Sunday dawned bright and clear. Not a cloud in the sky, Joshua thought as he walked to the barn to milk the cow. Do You not want us to go to church today, God? If it had been raining, maybe Matthew would've changed his mind. He shrugged and shook his head. As he finished milking the cow, a sudden thought came to him. That had been his first prayer since his argument with Matthew.

He climbed the ladder to the hayloft. "God, I am sorry I stayed angry at Matthew so long. It was wrong of me. Help me apologize to him and help him accept my apology, please. I have missed talking to You. I just didn't realize it until now." A slight smile crept up on his mouth as he tossed hay down to the horses before climbing down the ladder. "I've even missed talking to that bull-headed brother of mine." His smile grew even bigger.

He saw Matthew already headed for the kitchen door. He hurried to catch up with him. Breakfast waited! His stomach growled. Matthew opened the door and stepped inside. *Odd,* Joshua thought. *I don't smell anything cooking. What is going on?* Joshua ran into Matthew's back when Matthew came to a sudden stop in front of him.

"What is this?" Matthew asked from just inside the door. Joshua moved around Matthew to see what was happening. Leslie, Eliza, Robert, and Ruth sat at the kitchen table, a Bible open in front of them, and they held hands as they prayed together.

"Where is my breakfast?" Matthew demanded.

Leslie, Ruth, and the kids ignored him as they continued praying. Joshua watched them in admiration, his grin rapidly broadening to a full smile.

"I think Leslie and Ruth decided not to make breakfast this morning," Joshua said.

Matthew shot Joshua an angry look. "I can see that," he snapped. "What I want to know is why?"

Joshua shrugged. "They're probably tired of us staying mad at each other."

Matthew shook his head in frustration. Joshua grinned as he waited for confirmation from the silent foursome.

"What are you smiling about?" Matthew snapped.

"It is a wonderful day to be alive," he replied with a hint of joy in his voice. "I have decided that Ruth and I will stay here until the crops are in." He held up a hand for silence before Matthew could respond. "But, as soon as they're in, we are leaving."

Leslie and Ruth looked up in unison at Joshua's declaration.

Matthew glared at him. "Fine. Let's get out there then."

"Sorry for staying angry with you, Matthew."

Matthew grunted in reply as he headed to the door. Joshua followed reluctantly, flashing a wry smile at Leslie and Ruth.

Ruth smiled her encouragement. "I will try to get some food out to you soon so you don't starve."

Joshua laughed as he headed out to the field. Determined to make this Lord's Day a day of worship, he launched into song as he gathered his tools.

Joshua quickly discovered how hard it was to harvest wheat on an empty stomach. The day was hot and sticky, and Joshua was soon drenched in sweat. Since Matthew was unable to afford a new threshing machine, they worked the old-fashioned way: with scythes. Joshua preferred scythes anyway. Even on hot days like today he liked the rhythmic motion of swinging the scythe back and forth, back and forth, back and forth.

Today, he still found it soothing, but less than usual. His stomach was tight and empty. He hoped Ruth would make good on her promise to bring him something to eat. At least they had a bucket of water at the edge of the field. He glanced at Matthew without breaking his rhythm. Surely Matthew must be feeling the hunger pangs, too. Joshua sighed. He knew his brother's stubbornness too well. Matthew would never quit until it was all done or he collapsed in exhaustion.

Think about something other than your stomach, he scolded himself. Bible verses. That should work. He began quoting Bible verses in rhythm to his scythe. A grin started to appear on his face as he worked on putting the verses to simple tunes. He could get used to singing and quoting Scripture in time to the scythe. It certainly helped pass the time.

He reached the end of a row and looked back. His eyes narrowed. Was his scythe blade dull? The blade had left the wheat stems cut in jagged lines. He frowned as he put his thumb to the blade and shook his head in disbelief. It was dull. He had never had a blade get dull that fast.

As he started trudging toward the sharpening wheel, he noticed that Matthew was already there.

"Yours is dull, too?"

"We've used 'em a lot this week," Matthew said.

Joshua resisted the urge to roll his eyes at his brother's emotionless existence and shrugged. "I suppose, but I just checked this blade last night after we finished for the day. It shouldn't be this dull after just two rows." A mischievous look entered his eyes. "Unless you planted steel-stemmed wheat."

Matthew glared up at him. "Very funny, Joshua." Joshua observed the slightest hint of a smile in Matthew's eyes. *Would he actually get in a good mood? Or was the smile just my imagination? After all, the hint could have just been his exhaustion or pain or...anything really.*

Matthew slowly rose to his feet and plodded back to the field as Joshua moved into place to sharpen the scythe.

They worked at a steady pace for another couple of hours. Joshua sent a quick, worried glance up at the sky a time or two until he got too engrossed in his singing and work. He was singing his favorite hymn, "A Mighty Fortress Is Our God," when he heard a young voice join his. A grin spread on his face when he noticed Robert carrying a basket of food. His stomach growled in anticipation of the feast.

"Matthew!" Joshua yelled. "The food is here!"

Matthew stretched his back and rubbed his eyes as if tired. He grunted his acknowledgment. "I'm not hungry."

Joshua wondered if he could believe his ears. How was that possible? "Fine. Do whatever you want." He shook his head and jogged to meet up with Robert. Matthew was near them when Robert spoke up.

"Here's your food, Uncle Joshua. Dad, Mom said to tell you to look to the east. She thinks God is trying to tell you something." Still humming Martin Luther's hymn, Robert handed the basket to Joshua before skipping off.

Matthew turned with narrowed eyes. He swore under his breath.

Joshua shook his head at Matthew's unusually profane language and with reluctance he followed Matthew's gaze. Low in the horizon, but moving toward them at a rapid pace, were large, black clouds. Not dark gray—black as coal.

"Don't just stand there gawking!" Matthew snapped. "Let's finish harvesting before the storm hits."

Joshua stepped in front of his brother. "Matthew Brookings! Use the brain God gave you! If we continue harvesting, the rain will ruin the entire crop. We need to get Leslie, Ruth, and the kids out here to help us get the harvested wheat inside the barns."

Matthew's shoulders slumped and his eyes glazed over. Joshua sensed that something wasn't right. Matthew didn't respond with an offhand smart-aleck reply and he looked like he hadn't slept all night. Realization hit Joshua like a ton of bricks. "Matthew, did you sleep at all last night or did you come out here and try to harvest wheat in the dark?"

Matthew staggered. "We gotta get the wheat—" His exhaustion made his speech sound almost like he was drunk. Joshua made a quick, executive decision. He grabbed Matthew's arm and pulled him toward the house. "You are going to bed. I'll get the wheat in the barn for safekeeping."

To his amazement, Matthew didn't protest. Leslie looked up in surprise when they entered the house.

"Get him to bed and then all of you get out to the fields to help me with the wheat," Joshua ordered. "We need to get the wheat in the barns before the storm hits. I'll hitch the horses."

As he strapped the horses into their harnesses, he thanked God for Leslie. She did not ask unnecessary questions. Leslie, Ruth, Robert, Eliza, and Joshua worked at a pace beyond their years and natural abilities managing to get the wheat inside before the rains hit. The first sprinklings of rain chased after them as Joshua drove the last wagon of wheat into the barn. Looking out the kitchen window, they watched as the downpour began.

Monday dawned bright and cheery. Matthew came down for chores and looked mostly human that morning. As they put their boots on, Matthew spoke, "After breakfast, we'll head out to harvest the rest of the wheat."

Joshua stared at him, confusion etched into his face. "Didn't you hear the storm last night?"

Matthew's hand paused as it reached the doorknob. "What storm?"

Joshua shoved past him and opened the door. Matthew stared past Joshua and the barn to the wheat field.

"A bad hailstorm went through. I doubt if anyone around us has crops to harvest anymore. All we have is the wheat we have harvested the last few days. We were able to get it all inside before the rain started."

Matthew stared in disbelief at the thoroughly beaten fields. His face was a study in self-control. He let no emotion enter his face. He stepped past Joshua and headed to the barn.

Half an hour later, Joshua and Matthew sat silently eating their hotcakes with the family. Matthew had yet to say a word since hearing about the storm.

Joshua finished eating and was about to get up when Matthew's voice arrested his movement. "I have been very selfish these past few days." He paused, swallowing hard. "I needed that crop to pay for next year's crop. Because of that need, I pushed myself and others harder than I should've. Instead of trusting God, I trusted my own reasoning."

He looked across the table to where Ruth sat. "Ruth, you are turning into a lovely young woman. You may be only fifteen, but you have such a big heart, and you are not afraid to correct someone, even if they are twelve years older than you. Your note of encouragement and exhortation was just what I needed yesterday."

Ruth's eyes were filled with happy tears and a shy smile lit up her face as she dipped her head in silent acknowledgment.

Matthew turned his attention to his wife. "Leslie." His eyes were wet. "Leslie, you have been a faithful wife. Your gentle prodding and reminders this morning were the extra push I needed." He blinked rapidly before looking at Joshua.

"Joshua. I don't know what to say besides thank you. I know we are too much alike at times. Our wills butt against and into each other too often. This week is a living testament of that. Yesterday, I saw you grow up and grow past some of that. You were a much better man than I. Despite knowing that you were breaking the Sabbath, you obeyed my orders. You went above and beyond what was asked of you when you forced me into bed and got the wheat in the barns. Thank you."

Joshua watched Matthew gather his thoughts. "I have already asked God's forgiveness, and now I must ask yours. Can you? Will you all forgive me for everything I have done or failed to do the last few days?"

Ruth was the first to respond. She moved swiftly to her oldest brother and put her arms around his neck. "I forgave you days ago," she said in her quiet voice.

Leslie smiled softly. "As did I."

"And me," came two small voices.

Joshua laughed. "And I forgave you yesterday morning."

Matthew smiled, the relief evident on his face. "Thank you all! Now, I have one more thing to say before you all disappear." He grinned in satisfaction at the five eager faces. "Ruth and Joshua, you can leave as soon as you are ready and as soon as the stagecoach is available."

"Yippee!" Joshua shouted. "Can I go to the stage office right now?"

"No," Matthew stated. "I think we should let Ruth go."

Joshua felt a twinge of jealousy that Matthew would choose Ruth over him, but when he noticed Ruth's eyes glitter with joy, he knew his brother had seen something that made him think Ruth had wanted to go.

He knew that Ruth was a sensitive and shy girl. As the youngest of five siblings, all of whom were energetic and boisterous, Ruth often seemed out of place and out of mind. She was also very helpful. From a young age, she had always picked things up and helped her mother and her sisters, Martha and Esther, in any way she could.

Joshua was the closest to her in age at seventeen. Though still loud and boisterous, Joshua was the most subdued of the older four children and he was often the one most able to understand her unspoken desires. However, since moving in with Matthew, Matthew had begun picking up on them, too. Joshua was glad Matthew had seen this desire of hers.

"We should write Pa and Mother first so I can mail the letter telling them we are on our way," Ruth said quietly.

"I'll get the pen, ink, and paper," Joshua volunteered.

CHAPTER TWO

MAY 1868
STUART FARM
TENNESSEE

Iain Stuart made sure his son Jed knew how ashamed of and mad he was at him. His mother had died giving Jed life. The doctor had been unable to save her. Jed's da had loved his wife more than his life and hated his new son. Iain's hatred for Jed fermented and spread until they were both bitter toward each other. Jed's sister and brother were treated with some respect and a touch of love from Iain, but Jed received none of it. Instead, he got all the blame for everything.

The beatings came just about every day. As a boy, Jed tried to understand why he was beaten, but soon found it impossible. The only reason Jed could figure out was that his da hated him so much that he tried to beat him to death each day simply because he was still alive. He had learned to try to please his da from an early age. But the beatings still came.

Every night after a beating, Jed dreamed of the ways he could get back at his da. He knew he had to get away as soon as he had the strength and courage.

He bided his time and the day finally came. On Jed's fourteenth birthday, as he looked across the table at his da, he realized that he could look past the top of his da's head. This realization gave Jed the edge he needed.

Jed followed Iain out to do chores. Caleb had already gone to the field and Anna was cleaning up after breakfast.

It was finally time! "Da!" Jed stopped walking. Iain stopped and turned around. "We need ta talk," Jed said. Jed walked up to his da until he stood nose to nose. Iain glared at his son and Jed glared right back.

"What'd you want to talk aboot?" Iain asked, a threat in his voice.

"You," Jed said. "You'll never beat on me again."

Iain said nothing. Jed briefly wondered what he was thinking, but shoved the notion aside when he saw his da set his jaw and tense up.

"I'm leavin'," Jed hissed through clenched teeth as he spun on his boot heel to leave, but Iain, shaking with rage, grabbed his shoulder and threw a fist at his son's face. Jed raised his arm to block the punch and the two began trading blows.

Jed had the advantage. He was taller and more agile. The hatred and bitterness that he had been harboring for fourteen years came out through his fists. His da would find out what it was like to be beaten so badly you could barely walk. Jed didn't stop until his da lay on the ground, unmoving.

Jed stared at the mess he had made, gave his da one last kick, turned on his heel, and stormed to the house. He grabbed his father's army revolver off the porch and left everything behind. There would be no more farming, no more beatings, and no more family. He would make his own way.

The woods had always been Jed's friend. He often escaped into them and had learned much about how to survive there. If necessary, he could live off them for years. Whenever he was in the woods, he was content, even almost happy. Today he was even more happy and content because he knew he'd never go back. He would live in the woods and have nothing to do with humans ever again.

Jed strode forward with a purpose he had never felt before. As he worked his way into the woods, he took a deep breath, smelling the intoxicating, free air. His eyes remained ever alert as he let his feet carry him far away from his family. An abrupt notion occurred to him as he walked on. *Would his brother and sister miss him?* He dismissed the idea almost as soon as it came. They'd never done anything more than feed him and take care of his cuts and bruises.

He came to the edge of a steep embankment and hastily stumbled backwards. He crouched to look down at the road he had almost fallen onto. On the road he saw a stagecoach with a dead driver and shotgun guard. He shuddered at the sight of the dead men. Then he saw movement. Three men carried things to their horses while another moved a tree out of the road. He watched with growing curiosity as each of the men worked without talking, discussion, or apparent signals.

After they mounted their horses and the leader gave a signal to leave, Jed stood up to start on his way to freedom. The outlaws had already taken care of the bodies and he saw no reason to involve himself or his emotions in anything. Jed was about to turn away and continue working his way farther from his former home when one of the men saw him and yelled out, "Tom, thar's a stray!"

Jed stood frozen to the spot, staring down at the three men on horseback, unsure of what to do. These men had murdered the men driving the stage. Had he escaped his da just to be killed in cold blood for accidentally stumbling on the robbery? Jed felt the blood drain from his face and his hands began to shake. Should he bolt? *No, that'd make 'em shoot me for sure.*

Jed stood with his arms hanging limply against his sides. He glanced down at the leader and worked up his courage to talk to the man.

"What're you gonna do with me?"

"You with th' stage?" Tom asked.

"No, I ain't."

Tom's eyes narrowed.

"If I were with the stage, you think I'd be standing here jawin' with you? Nah, I'd have shot you all by now." Jed's heart beat like a herd of spooked wild horses and his mouth was dry. He could hardly believe that his voice sounded so steady and confident.

Boy and man stared at each other for a long moment. Jed could have sworn it was the longest minute of his life.

The outlaw leader spurred his horse around the embankment, continuing on until his horse's nose was touching the bottom of Jed's chest.

"Why're you here, Boy?"

Jed jutted his chin out. "I ran away from home and headed this way, nearly falling down the embankment. I've only been here for a few minutes." He paused. "You really know how to handle your men, Sir."

Tom looked at him with narrowed eyes. Jed wondered what was going through the man's mind.

Jed stared up at Tom and he stared back at Jed. The staring match lasted a full two minutes.

"What's yer name, Boy?"

Jed pondered the question. *Should I give my real name or come up with a new one?* Not having any ideas offhand, he made his decision. "Jed Stuart."

Tom nodded. "What were you plannin' on doing after runnin' away, Jed?"

Jed shrugged, a bored expression on his face. He tried his hardest not to show any of the fear he felt. "I figgered I'd live off the woods."

Tom lifted his eyebrows. "Would ya now? And just how long d'ya think you would've lasted?" He shook his head. "I don't cotton ta takin' charity cases, but I can't have you headin' straight for town neither. So either I gotta shoot you or take you with me and the boys."

Jed's throat went even dryer and his heart sank to his stomach. Tom seemed to be waiting for something. Jed wasn't sure what, so resigning himself to whatever fate Tom chose, he squared his shoulders and lifted his head to meet Tom's unfaltering gaze. The right corner of Tom's mouth twitched with such a small motion, Jed almost missed it. He had a feeling that was as close to a smile as he would ever see on Tom's face.

"Dustin!" Tom yelled. "Bring over the extry horse. We got us a new boy to train in the ways of the outlaw."

"You got it, Tom!"

Tom kept Jed busy doing all the grunt work. He took care of the horses, gathered firewood, cooked, washed clothes, and hauled water. When nobody was around, Jed practiced with his revolver, knowing that practicing was the only way he could be the fastest draw around. Tom insisted he be a good shot with a rifle, so he also practiced with one of the rifles.

One day, just months before Jed turned fifteen, Tom approached him, a grim look on his face as he held a rifle in his hands. "Jed?"

"Yeah, Tom?"

Tom turned the rifle over in his hands. "I'm givin' ya a very important job. We're gonna rob a stagecoach today. I need ya to sit where I tell ya and shoot the shotgun guard off the coach. Got it?"

Jed nodded even as his throat constricted and his stomach churned. Could he really kill a man?

"I've seen ya shoot, Boy. I know ya can shoot from a distance and draw fast when needed. This is the most important job I could give ya. Ya miss and the whole thing could go wrong. Got it, Boy?"

Jed gulped. Had Tom seen him practicing his fast draw? Jed took the rifle Tom handed him. He put one hand around the barrel and looked up at Tom with a determined glint in his eyes. It was time for him to prove himself to this group of men.

As Jed walked away, he heard Lefty ask Tom, "Why're you givin' the kid that job? It's his first robbery. His first time doin' anything illegal."

Tom's voice was hard and full of anger. "I'm aware of that," he snapped. "I've seen Jed shoot. He's better'n any of us. He may be green, but he's still the best for the job."

Jed turned his head in time to see Tom stalking off and Lefty shaking his head, a disbelieving look on his face. Jed's determination grew. He knew now that this would be his one and only chance to prove himself.

So a man would die to give him that chance—what did that matter to him? If he wanted to make it in the world of outlaws, he'd have to do some killing. Jed shivered despite the warmth of the autumn sun. He clenched his jaw and straightened his spine to rigid attention, all the while hardening his heart to the man he would be killing in a matter of hours.

The sun arched its way to the western lands as they worked their way to the site of the robbery. Tom put Jed on a hill above the road where he would have a perfect shot at the guard. Dustin and Lefty waited on the other side of the road and Tom stood in the middle of the road, rifle cradled in his arms.

When the time came, he took the guard down with one shot. He felt exhilarated and disturbed at the same time. *I just ended a man's life.*

But he had no time to think about it. He needed to help unload the money box and get the stage off the road. They took the horses with them and dumped the stage down the side of the road and out of sight.

Once they got to the hideout, Lefty went up to Jed. "Jed, I gotta admit, I was a bit surprised when I heard Tom was giving you that job. But after I seen what you done, and how well you done it, I'd trust you with my life."

Dustin nodded his assent as Tom came up and slapped Jed's shoulder. "Ya did good, Kid. Just don't get cocky. Ya get cocky and it could cost yers and others' lives."

Jed dipped his head. "Yes, Sir." His heart swelled with pride as he went to work. He was finally being accepted for who he was.

A few weeks later, Tom decided it was time to go into town and get a few drinks. Jed came with, but as the son of a Scotsman who was often drunk, he had never liked the idea of drinking. To keep up appearances, Jed slowly sipped a beer, all the while keeping a sharp eye out on everything and everybody. Tom had just finished what he had said was his last drink when a commotion began. Jed watched as Lefty swung his fist at another man's jaw. Tom jerked to his feet; he wobbled as he went to try to stop the fight, but Jed had already seen the problem and, being steadier on his feet, Jed was halfway across the room before Tom even got out of his chair.

Jed stepped between the two men, an arm outstretched to each of them, separating them as much as he could. "Calm down—"

"Stay outta this, Boy!" the man spat.

Jed turned his back on the man and spoke to Lefty. "Lefty, let's get going."

"That man insulted me!" Lefty protested.

"Don't matter," Jed said flatly. "We don't want no trouble. This would be trouble."

A firm hand grabbed Jed's shoulder and spun him around. The man, now in front of him, was livid. "You don't turn your back on me, Boy." His eyes narrowed as he eyed the revolver on Jed's hip. "Can you use that gun, Boy?"

Jed looked the man full in the face with eyes full of hatred. "Yeah," he hissed, eyes narrowing. "I can use it."

"It's time to teach you a lesson then, Boy. Then your friend can leave." The man's evil laugh rang through the silent saloon.

Men scattered as Jed took a few quick strides backwards. Jed and the man stood facing each other. They watched each other carefully. Jed saw the man's hand waver with slight movement and Jed drew his gun, aiming it with a quick and sure confidence bred by much practice. The other man's gun didn't even have time to clear leather before his body fell to the floor.

Stunned silence reigned for a few breathless seconds. Then mayhem and noise broke loose.

"Did you see—?"

"I never seen anybody draw that fast!"

"He's just a kid—"

Jed looked at Lefty, who stared back at him in disbelief. Tom staggered over with Dustin at his side and the four left town. None of them wanted to be questioned by the sheriff.

The next morning, a subdued Tom sat at the rough table in their hideout.

"Jed? What you done last night is goin' to earn you the label of a gunfighter."

Jed looked up, then back down at his plate. He shrugged. "So?"

"Other men'll come hunting you down to test you. Some men will want to hire you to kill people for them. You prepared to do that?"

"If it's a way to get money, I'll do it. I'm already an outlaw, may's well go the whole way."

Tom nodded and nothing more was said.

As the years passed, Jed came to love his new life. With Tom and the gang, he grew from a gangly boy into a full-grown man. He filled out and grew taller; he even grew a beard, something his da would have hated. Jed stayed with Tom and his gang most of the time, but once in a while he did some gun-fighting. Jed enjoyed the feeling of being accepted for who he was instead of who he wasn't. He could live this way his whole life, or so he thought.

CHAPTER THREE

OCTOBER 1875

David and Matthew lifted the trunk on top of the stagecoach. Was it really possible that they could be leaving? To Joshua it seemed like the most wonderful dream ever. Everything was packed, the whole family was there to see him and Ruth off, everything seemed perfect. Except for the fact that they would be leaving so many friends and family members behind.

Their parents had finally been able to save enough money to start building their lifelong dream: a horse ranch out West. The only regret Daniel and Harriet Brookings had was that they couldn't bring all of their children with them. The family had always been so close, not just in proximity, but in friendship. Joshua knew their parting would be hardest on Ruth. She was shy and did not make friends easily. Her best friends were her sisters, Esther and Martha.

Esther gave Joshua a big hug. "Take care of our little sister, Joshua."

Martha's eyes were full of tears. "Joshua, you are her only protector out there until you get to Pa and Ma. Keep her safe."

Joshua nodded and swallowed hard as tears threatened to spring to his eyes. "With God's help, I will."

David and Benjamin, Esther's and Martha's husbands, stood aloof from the group. They were quiet farmers who were hard to get close to and didn't say much. Ruth gave each of them a hug before turning to her sisters.

"Take care of yourselves and those new babies," she said. Esther and Martha laughed with her.

"You should know you don't even need to say that," Esther scolded with a twinkle in her eye.

"I know, but I felt like saying it anyway," Ruth teased back.

Robert and Eliza ran to Ruth. "Don't go!" they pleaded.

Ruth squatted on her heels and hugged them both close. "I have to, Darlings. Your grandpa and grandma need me out on their new ranch. I need you to stay here and take good care of your mama and papa for me."

Robert pulled back and looked her in the eyes. "Really?" His eyes were wide and curious. "How would we do that?"

"By listening to them and obeying them. And by helping as much as possible. With Joshua leaving, your father will need a lot more help from you, Robert. He will need your help with the chores, the planting, the weeding, and the harvest. Eliza, with me gone your mother will need you to gather the eggs, feed the chickens, and help with the cooking, cleaning, and laundry." She looked them in the eyes as she talked to them.

"Will that help us from missing you so much?" Eliza asked.

"If you are so busy you don't have time to think, yes, it will. I expect that you will still miss us, but I do think that helping out as much as you can will keep you from missing us as much."

Ruth stood up and found Leslie staring at her with an awed look in her eyes. "Thank you," she whispered. "I will miss you terribly, Little Sister."

Ruth melted into her sister-in-law's arms. "I will miss you, too."

"Thank you for comforting the children...again." Leslie smiled through her tears. "I will have to write to you for advice on how to handle some of their petty complaints."

Matthew laughed. "A grown woman writing a fifteen year old girl for advice on raising children?" He shook his head in amusement before pulling Ruth into his arms. "I'm gonna miss your calming influence and encouraging words, Sis."

"I will write to you," Ruth promised, her voice muffled by Matthew's shirt.

Matthew let go of her. "I'll count on that." His voice was gruff with emotion.

Joshua hung back and watched his family say goodbye to Ruth before moving in to say his goodbyes.

Joshua held his hand out to Matthew. Matthew's grip was strong and he slapped Joshua's shoulder with his free hand. Joshua's voice cracked as he looked into his brother's face. "I don't know what to say. I don't know how best to say goodbye. And thank you."

Their eyes met and the unspoken words and thoughts were communicated. "You're welcome," Matthew said, swallowing hard. "Thank you for all of your help."

Joshua nodded as he let go of Matthew. "Leslie."

"I'll miss you, Joshua," Leslie said.

Joshua hugged her tight. "I'll miss you, too. You have been a wonderful sister-in-law and hostess."

"Thank you. You take care of yourself and Ruth on the journey. You never know what you might run into."

"Yes, Ma'am. I'll do that."

David cleared his throat. "Keep your gun handy. I doubt you'll need it, but you never know." He paused, looking past Joshua. "I'll miss our talks together, even though you always did most of the talkin'." He smiled.

Joshua smiled as he shook David's hand. "I'll miss our talks, too. Take good care of my sister and your kids."

He shook hands with Benjamin, hugged his two sisters, and then turned to Eliza and Robert. He squatted down and stretched his arms wide. Robert barreled into him with Eliza following close behind. Joshua almost fell flat on his back, barely managing to keep himself balanced. He whispered his goodbyes and last-minute advice to his niece and nephew.

"Robert, you remember what Ruth said, help your pa and ma. You also need to keep your sister safe." Robert's head thudded into Joshua's shoulder a few times as he nodded his head. "Eliza, you also need to remember what Ruth said. You are a beautiful young lady; stay close to God and you will grow up to be just like your mama."

Eliza sniffled. "I will. Goodbye, Uncle Joshua."

"Goodbye, Sweetheart." Joshua stood up and brushed the dust off his tan pants. Not that it would matter in an hour. He knew stagecoaches made people look like they had just been through a sandstorm.

"All passengers to board now!" a loud voice announced.

"I guess that's us, Ruthie."

Ruth looked up into the sparkling eyes of her brother. "Yes, I guess it is," she echoed timidly.

Benjamin stood next to the door and helped Ruth into the stage. Joshua was just two steps behind her. As Joshua sat down, Benjamin shut the door and told the driver they were both in the stage. Ruth and Joshua waved their hands out of the windows while the driver started the horses going. They kept waving until they could no longer see the town.

"Well, we're off," Joshua said with a sigh as he leaned back against the cloth-covered seat.

Ruth nodded, still looking out the window. "Yes, we are. Let's just pray the trip goes smoothly."

They bounced along all day with a few quick stops along the way. At the end of the day, they halted at a stage stop, ate a hot meal, and slept in lumpy beds. Joshua was so tired he didn't even realize that the beds were not comfortable. As long as he could sleep in a bed, he did not care.

The next few days, the scenery changed gradually as they traveled through Illinois and into Missouri. Joshua had expected adventure, but this was pure monotony. They would eat breakfast at daybreak, get in the stage a little later, eat lunch sometime during the drive, break for a quick breather while the horses were changed, pull into another stage station an hour after the sun went down, eat a quick supper, fall into bed, repeat.

So much for adventure, Joshua thought. *This is downright boring! Even thinking about it makes me tired.*

There were a few things those first days that were interesting. First, they got to know the driver and guard fairly well after their few quick meals together. Joshua found out that their driver's name was Gage Bradford.

After some gentle prodding by Ruth, Mr. Bradford opened up about himself.

"I always loved horses," he said with a slight smile playing at the edges of his mouth. "I grew up in Arizona on a cattle ranch. I watched the stage every day as it passed my house. I always envied the driver as he handled the horses with such care.

"As soon as Father gave me leave, I applied to become a stagecoach driver. I worked hard those first couple o' years. I didn't start out driving; first I started out with the horses, taking care of them— grooming them, getting them in shape for their next journey.

"During that first year, I met Esperanza, a beautiful Spanish girl. I started courting her and we were married just before I started driving for the company. After a year of marriage, I was transferred to this line."

"Do you and Esperanza have any children?" Joshua asked.

"We have three. Jonny, Davy, and Maria." His face had a wistful expression. "That's the only thing I don't like about this job. It keeps me away from my family."

The room grew quiet as they all contemplated their own separations.

The next night, Ruth asked the guard about his family. His answer was short and simple.

"I got no family. They was killed a while back. Never had any use for marriage. I am good at usin' a gun, so I decided to hire out to sit on a stagecoach, keep the driver awake, and keep the stage safe from Injuns, robbers, and wild animals."

Both men were perfect gentlemen, but Mr. Bradford was definitely the most friendly. Joshua couldn't help but wonder what kind of life the guard, Mr. Larson, had as a child. How was his family killed? How old was he when it happened? What had he done after they were killed? He wanted to ask Mr. Larson all of those questions and more, but something in Mr. Larson's eyes warned him not to ask.

Halfway through Nebraska, the stagecoach arrived at its planned stop almost an hour earlier than anticipated. Since it was sunny but not too hot, Joshua, Ruth, and Gage Bradford decided to wander the small property to stretch their legs.

After a while, Mr. Bradford stopped walking and leaned against the fence to watch the horses in the corral. Joshua joined him at the fence and Ruth walked down a little farther to the corner.

They all stood there watching the horses graze and frolic. A few minutes passed in silence until Ruth broke in, "Mr. Bradford, what is the funniest thing your kids have ever done?"

Joshua glanced sideways and saw a litany of emotions sweep across Gage Bradford's face: surprise, humor, longing, remembrance, desire, joy...

"Hmm, let me think on that a moment." Mr. Bradford had a mischievous twinkle in his eyes as he tipped his head back and looked up at the cloudless blue sky.

"I believe this story happened when Jonny was eight. So, just about seven years ago." He paused as he stared ahead into the distant landscape. "Yes, that would have to be the funniest.

"Jonny has always been our mischievous child. He gets the other two into the worst trouble. The good thing is that he is always there and willing to get them out of the trouble. Esperanza and I have gotten to the point where we know Jonny will drag his sister and brother into some funny, harmless, but crazy antics. We don't even worry about it anymore."

Mr. Bradford's grin widened as he bent down to pick a long blade of grass. Putting the grass between his teeth, he leaned his side against the fence to face Ruth. "The funniest thing my kids ever did was to play a prank on their parents and have it backfire on them." He chuckled at the memory. "Instead of pranking us, they ended up pranking themselves.

"Jonny had the brilliant idea of switching the salt and sugar on the table. That way, when I went to put a little sugar in my coffee, I would end up with salty coffee instead of sweetened coffee. It would've worked great, except that we were almost out of sugar in the sugar bin. Davy's birthday was the next day and Esperanza baked him a cake. But, she needed another half cup of sugar, so she took the sugar bowl off the table and used a half cup of what she thought was sugar from the sugar bowl."

Joshua could hardly keep the boiling laughter from bursting forth. Glancing at his sister, he could tell she knew where this story was going.

Mr. Bradford was a great storyteller. If it wasn't for the twinkle in his eyes and the laugh lines around his mouth, Joshua would almost believe the man had no emotions at all.

"Now, in our family, it is tradition for the birthday boy to choose who gets to take the first bite out of the cake. Davy had been watching his mother bake the cake the night before. He also knew what Jonny had done. After all, he had helped Jonny do the switch by holding the sugar bowl while Jonny poured the salt in.

"Davy has always been a smart boy."

Ruth cocked her head to the side and interrupted, "How old was Davy at the time?"

Gage smiled. "Davy was only three, but very bright for his age." After a brief pause, he continued. "After watching his mother put a half cup of salt in the cake, Davy knew Jonny needed to be the first to take a bite of the cake. Davy blew out his three candles, Esperanza cut the cake, and I asked Davy who he wanted to give the honor of the first bite to.

"Without missing a beat, without a smirk, smile, or any giveaway, Davy said, 'Jonny.' Jonny grinned and cut a large bite out of his piece, stabbed it with his fork, and stuffed it into his mouth, chewing vigorously." Gage Bradford cleared his throat and tried to wipe the grin off his face with his hand.

"Jonny chewed and swallowed the entire bite, but the look on his face was priceless. He was thoroughly disgusted with the taste and grabbed for his glass of milk to wash the cake down and get the flavor out of his mouth.

"As soon as the milk was swallowed, Jonny choked out, 'What did you do to this cake, Mama?' Esperanza looked at him in astonishment. She had no idea what he meant. Before she could speak, Davy saved us all. 'She ran outta sugar in the bin and used the sugar in the bowl, Jonny.' The accusing look Davy had on his face caused me to grab the sugar bowl and taste the substance inside. 'How much sugar did you put in the cake from this bowl?' I asked my wife.

"'Half a cup. Why?' she asked. I looked at Jonny. Jonny's eyes were wide and guilt and horror were written all over his face. All I said was, 'Somebody put salt in the sugar bowl.' Esperanza's eyes went wide. 'You mean I put a half cup of salt in that cake?' Davy, Maria, and I burst out laughing. Esperanza eventually joined in the laughter, but Jonny didn't."

Mr. Bradford shook his head with a grin plastered from ear to ear. "It took months for Jonny to touch either sugar or salt again."

Joshua gave up trying to contain his laughter. Ruth and Mr. Bradford joined him until they all had tears streaming down their cheeks.

"I wish I'd been there," Joshua gasped. "I can see that happening with Matthew and me. Too bad we never thought of that."

"Can you imagine Mother's reaction?" Ruth asked. "She would be horrified that she had allowed that to happen in her kitchen."

"What about Pa's reaction?" Joshua burst into another fit of laughter. "He would have been laughing the hardest of all of us."

Gage Bradford wiped the tears off his face. "I surely do miss my family. Sometimes I wish I could find another good job so I could see them more."

Ruth walked over to Mr. Bradford and put a comforting hand on his arm. "I'm sure you're doing the best you can and that is all that can be asked of you. You care for your family and you take care of them. I can tell you are a good father, even if you are gone a lot."

Joshua watched his sister with envy. She always knew exactly what to say.

"Maybe once Pa has the ranch started, we could hire you on to help take care of the horses."

Gage Bradford shook his head and grinned through the sadness in his eyes. "You two are very special young people. I'll have to keep your offer in mind. Thank you, Joshua. And thank you, Ruth."

A clanging sound reached their ears. "I'll bet that means supper's ready," Joshua said. "I'm all for it. I'm starved!"

CHAPTER FOUR

APRIL 1870
NEBRASKA

As the months passed by, Tom's gang varied in size. At times there were up to six men. Other times there were less. No one ever left for good, unless they were killed. Sometimes they left to do a different job. For Jed, that meant he would occasionally go off to be a hired gun.

Jed had been with Tom's gang for over two years when he started noticing a change. For two years, he had been the lackey, doing whatever he was told to do. After being given that first job of killing the shotgun guard, and then getting in a gunfight, Jed started changing. He noticed that something was different, but could not figure out what it was. He began to grow more confident in his skills, more hardened to killing, more bitter about his lot in life.

The first time he noticed his less than subtle change he was on his way back to the small cabin he shared with the gang when he heard some of the men talking.

"You got the goods?" Carson asked him.

"Would I have come back without them?"

Carson grinned. "Not if you wanted to live more than two seconds after comin' back."

Tyree butted into the conversation. "There ain't no way you'd be alive to know that. He's lots faster than you."

Milton guffawed. "He's got a point, Carson. A very valid point."

Jed narrowed his eyes. "What'cha guys talkin' about?"

"Your speed and aim with a gun," Tom said. "They've seen how good you are." Tom's voice had an extra sharp bite to it as he glared at Jed.

"When'd they see me shooting?" Jed asked. "I haven't drawn and shot in front of the gang in years."

Tyree eyed Jed, his pupils narrowing. "Word gets 'round. Word is on the street that yer faster'n most. Yer the man to hire if they need a fast gun."

"How'd that happen?" Jed was confused. He had only hired out three times since the incident in the saloon.

Milton leaned his chair back on its back legs, crossing his arms over his chest. "Well, let's see here. You're only sixteen right now. You outgunned Cassidy Jones—reportedly one of the best guns in his time—when you were but fourteen; you've successfully taken care of one job that would've made a hardened gunfighter blanch. Oh yeah, and you've also helped to stop a range war. Out here—word from the East might be a mite slow in coming—but word about the newest, youngest, best gunfighter? That news'll spread like wildfire. And it has."

Jed stared at Milton, his chest constricting. Even as he wondered how he could have been so oblivious, he started getting the feeling that he had finally done it. He had far exceeded his da's expectations. His chest puffed out slightly and a small grin played at his mouth.

"You could be right," Jed said. "I guess I just hadn't thought about it before."

Milton grinned and slammed his chair down on all fours as he stood up. "Me? I'd follow you any day, anywhere. You wanna go to Hades and back, I'll go with ya."

Jed glanced around the yard at the gang members, his eyes finally settling on Tom. Tom glared alternately between him and Milton. Jed wondered what he was thinking.

"I'm still the leader," Tom said. "Nothin's goin' ta change that."

Milton's head snapped down and up in a quick motion. "Sure, Tom, I realize that. I was just sayin'—"

"I know what you were sayin'," Tom growled. "You were sayin' you'd rather follow Jed than me. That's fine. Once fate catches up with me, you can follow him. In the meantime, I'll lead."

"Yeah, Tom. I know tha—"

"Shut up, Milton," Carson snapped. "Can't ya see you're just making him madder?"

Milton's eyebrows glowered together. "'Madder' isn't the right word," he mumbled to himself. "I'm not even sure it is a word."

Jed snapped out of his surprise, walked into the cabin, and dropped his packages on the table. As he stood alone in the middle of the cabin, he stared at the blank log wall. *I may be a good gunhand, but I'm certainly not looking to take over the gang. That will not happen on my watch. At least not yet. Tom is the best leader for this group of men. I'm too young to be a leader. Milt should've kept his mouth shut.* Jed clenched his jaw and ground his teeth. Now he would have to watch his back even around camp.

Two days later, Jed was still treading lightly around camp. He saw Tyree and Carson shooting at tin cans and shook his head in disgust. They could hardly hit the broadside of a barn from twenty feet away. Tyree and Carson were new recruits. After breaking the law out East, they'd escaped to the relative safety of the West. Jed was still watching them ten minutes later when Tom came up behind him.

"What do we do with those two numbskulls?" Tom asked.

"I'm not sure, Boss. Is there any hope we could teach 'em to shoot better?" Jed turned his head around to look at Tom.

Tom grimaced before letting out a humorless laugh. "Doubt it." His eyes shifted in Jed's direction. "You wanna try?"

Jed shrugged. "I could try. I can't make any guarantees."

"If they can even hit one in every ten cans, that'd be better than what they're doin' now."

Jed's lips curved up slightly around his peach fuzz. "You got it, Boss." Jed strode forward to start the shooting lessons.

Two hours later, Carson could hit one in every five cans he aimed at. Tyree hit one in every eight. Jed was reluctant in his satisfaction with their progress, but knew they would only get better with practice.

Three days later, Jed had an opportunity to see Tyree and Carson in action. He was optimistic that their new gun skills would be put to good use.

The gang of five arrived at the robbery site an hour before the stage was expected. Jed was put in the lead position as usual and the others were bunched together in a group where the stage was supposed to stop. There were no passengers on this stage and Jed was thankful for that. It was bad enough that they would have to kill the driver and shotgun guard.

Jed began his ritual of detaching his mind from what his body would be doing. He made his mind go blank. No thoughts. No pesky conscience. He stared at the road stretching ahead of him. His eyes barely registered the dirt, the wagon, buggy, and stage tracks, the old hoof prints.

A cloud of oncoming dust caught his eyes. The stage was on its way. Ten minutes later, Jed had his rifle resting in his shoulder and the hammer pulled back, and he worked on setting his aim. The stage was just coming into sight and Jed put his finger in the trigger guard. He squeezed the trigger just as his ears registered a startled cry from behind him. *Tyree,* Jed thought. *He's gonna get us all killed.*

Jed cursed as he saw his bullet miss its target and the guard lift his rifle, ready to shoot. Jed turned and raced for the rest of the gang.

"You missed," Tom stated.

"I did," Jed said.

Tom turned to Tyree. "As you messed up his aim, you'll be the one to go out there to stop the stage." Tyree blanched but nodded and ran into the road.

Tom shifted his attention to Carson. "You! Get behind that tree and shoot the first guard down before he gets to Tyree. Milton!"

"Yeah, Tom?" Milton asked.

"Get yerself outta here," Tom ordered. "We'll not be needing you until the money box is off the stage."

"Will do." Milton scurried a safe distance away.

"Jed, you sit tight here while Ty and Carson take care o' this," Tom demanded. "We'll stay here as reserves in case those two can't finish the job right."

Jed nodded and watched the road. The stage barreled toward Tyree and Carson with the speed brought on by panicked horses. Jed knew the instant the guard saw Tyree. He tried to yell at Tyree, but the guard was too fast. Tyree was dead before he even had a chance to get a look at the man who killed him.

Carson's gun went off and Jed saw the driver's body slump over in the driver's box. The guard used the driver's body for cover and searched the woods for Carson.

Jed saw Carson fumbling with his gun and knew the man was a dead man before he even heard the gun go off. Jed didn't wait for orders; he whipped his rifle into position and killed the guard.

Tom said nothing about the two dead gang members. He nodded at Jed, a silent commendation of his quick action. Milton and Jed worked together to dig a single shallow grave. All four bodies were rolled, dragged, and dumped into the grave and then covered up as best as they could manage. Tom loaded the gold and cash from the money box into the saddlebags before slapping the horses and getting them headed down the road.

Despite two of the gang members being dead, Tom seemed happy with the results. Jed returned to the hideout an hour later, moody and depressed. All those hours spent teaching Tyree and Carson how to shoot and it was wasted just because Tom wanted the money from the strongbox. Life had a way of confusing a man at times.

"I'm goin' to the woods for a while. I'll be back later," Jed announced to Tom.

Tom put a heavy hand on his shoulder. "What do you think you're doin'?"

Jed turned, his eyes flashing fire. "I gotta be alone for a while to let off some steam. Let me go or I may just blow up in here." His voice grated through his clenched teeth. Jed stared into Tom's eyes for a few more seconds before shrugging Tom's hand off his shoulder, spinning on his heel, and stomping into the woods.

Jed crashed carelessly through the woods until he came to the clearing he had found weeks before when they had first arrived at the hideout. Bursting into the clearing, Jed drew his pistols and starting shooting at imaginary foes: a flower, a bee buzzing from flower to flower, a squirrel. Anything that moved. Once his pistols were empty, he reloaded them and put one in each of the twin holsters on his hips.

His breath came hot and furious in and out of his chest, blowing past his lips, making them tingle and chapped. His mind started repeating Tom's last warning. *Be careful out there, the Sioux live in this area. Be careful out there, the Sioux live in this area.*

Jed scowled at the surrounding landscape, his eyes searching for any sign of movement. Seeing none, he allowed his thoughts to continue. *Why? What was the purpose behind all the death? Why did Tom send Tyree and Carson on what he knew was a suicide mission? They were practically still city slickers. Why would God allow all this to happen?*

"I hate You, God! Why do You keep taking people away from me? Why make me waste so much time with Tyree and Carson when You knew they would die today? I hate You! I hate you, too, Da! You are worse than God. At least God only took people away; you tried to take me away. I hate all of you."

His breath came in short gasps as he stood ramrod straight at the edge of the clearing. The sun was setting before Jed's brain told him he needed to move. *Maybe I should just abandon the gang,* he thought. Shaking his head, he dismissed the thought. *I don't have any food or money; I'd never make it.*

You were going to do it once, remember?

Jed blew out a burst of air from his nose. *Don't remind me.* He turned around and made his way back to the camp and the small gang he was a part of.

"Jed!" A familiar voice accosted him as he reached the cabin. "I was wonderin' where you'd gone off to."

Jed looked up from the ground, looking around for the man to go with the voice. "Lefty?" he asked.

"The one and only."

"What're you doin' here?"

"I told Tom I'd come back and here I am," Lefty replied.

Jed shook his head. "With perfect timing as usual."

Lefty looked at him blankly. "What?"

"We just lost two members of the gang."

Lefty's jaw dropped. "Two?"

"Carson and Tyree." Jed's voice was flat and emotionless.

"Huh. Not bookworm Milton?" Lefty asked.

"No, Milton is still very much alive. For now."

"Yeah. He'll get himself killed one of these days. A scholar should never become an outlaw." Lefty shook his head as he caught sight of Milton. "Speaking of—"

Jed looked past Lefty to see Milton reading a book while he walked from the cabin to the outhouse. "He just saw two of his gang members get killed and he's in there reading?"

Lefty looked back at Jed. "And what were you doing? Milt likes to read, so he'll read when troubled. We all got our rituals for relieving tension. You still shoot up trees when you're tense and disturbed, right? Well, Milt's way is readin'." Lefty shrugged as Jed stared at him, doubt in his eyes.

Jed shook his head trying to get the fog to clear out of his head. "Why're you here, Lefty?"

"I ran into an ol' friend of mine after runnin' from the law agin. Since we was in the area and needed a place to lay low, I thought we might see what was happenin' here." Lefty jerked his left thumb over his shoulder. "Garrett's in there talkin' to Tom."

Jed nodded. He was about to speak when Tom shouted from the cabin.

"Jed! Git in here!"

Jed raised an eyebrow at Lefty as he trudged into the cabin. The inside was dark with only a slit of sunlight that came in from the open door. Jed stood in the doorway for a minute to let his eyes adjust to the stark contrast.

"Jed, this is Garrett." Tom motioned to the man standing by the cold fireplace. "He's joinin' the gang." Tom turned to Garrett. "Garrett, this is Jed. He's my right-hand man. Listen ta him if you wanna survive."

Jed blinked his eyes and straightened. *I'm Tom's right-hand man? Since when?*

Tom dismissed Garrett and stared at Jed as Garrett walked out the door.

"A bit surprised, are you?" Tom questioned. He folded into the closest chair. "After Milton's outburst t'other day, I figgered I may as well make it official."

"Thank you, Sir," Jed stammered.

Tom waved his hand. "Stop with the 'sir' stuff, Jed. We've been partners over two years. Yer a man now, not a kid. Act and talk like one."

"Yes, Sir...I mean Tom. I'll try ta remember." Jed was desperate to get out of the small cabin. He felt like the walls were collapsing in on him, caving his chest in with them.

Tom sat still, staring sightlessly out the filthy window. Jed started backing toward the door with slow, heavy steps.

"You can go now, Jed." Tom's voice had a strange tone to it, but Jed didn't stop to question it. He turned and darted for the doorway. Once he was outside, Jed gasped in big breaths of air.

I'm second-in-command? Jed wondered. Then the realization hit him. *I'm second-in-command! Just two years in th' gang and I'm second!* Jed wandered into the woods putting one foot in front of another, moving steadily in no particular direction.

As he walked, his mind wandered through his past, among dark thoughts about his life with his da and siblings. He stumbled through the woods trying to flee the memories of home. The beatings, the complacency of his siblings, the comforting of his sister—always as an afterthought to the beatings.

He paused for air and forced his mind to think about the last two years. Two years in which he had finally been accepted. Two years in which he had found a reason to live. Two years in which he had honed his skills to the point that, at the young age of sixteen, he was the right-hand man of an outlaw leader.

His pace slowed as his thoughts calmed him. *It's high time that someone saw me for who I am. I can finally prove to people that I can really do this. I can be the leader Milton believes I am. I will be the leader Tom needs!* He stopped and looked up into the trees. "You hear that, Da? I'm provin' you wrong. Again."

Daylight had faded before Jed turned back to the outlaw camp. As he reached the clearing that held the cabin, he stopped and closed his eyes for mere seconds. When he opened them, he took a deep breath and strode into camp to start his new official position.

OCTOBER 1875
WYOMING TERRITORY

One Saturday evening in mid-October, four men sat around the small log cabin: Tom, Jed, Garrett, and Lefty. Tom looked up from oiling his bridle. His eyes were hard as flint.

"There be a stage comin' through near here in three days. It's got some money on it. We're takin' it."

"Passengers?" Lefty asked.

"Two."

Jed's eyes continued to stare into the mesmerizing flames. "Men or women?"

"How would I know?" Tom stormed. "I was lucky ta get what I got!"

Jed's eyes widened and he looked over at Tom, holding his hands up in surrender. "Sorry, I thought that mayb—"

"You thought?" Tom yelled. He stood up and advanced a step nearer to Jed. "I am the one s'pose ta think! Not you!"

Jed swallowed hard. "Right." Tom had always been short-tempered, but lately he had been worse.

Jed shook his head, noticing that Tom was still staring at him. Then his hard gaze turned to the room in general. "For this robbery we will jest take the money from the strongbox and the valybles from the passengers. As our normal practice when passengers are on board, we will try to ride off without a shot."

"Why're we taking a stage with passengers?" Lefty asked.

"We need the money. It's been months since our last robbery and this is the first stage in a long time to pass this way and still be carryin' money."

They all nodded their agreement. In the past, they had only robbed stages carrying money, not passengers, but on occasion they made an exception.

After a moment of thoughtful silence, Garrett spoke. "Why don't we rob stages with passengers?"

"Too many witnesses," Jed answered. "The fewer people that see us the better."

"Why not just shoot 'em?" Garrett narrowed his eyes in confusion.

Lefty punched him in the shoulder. "That's obvious. Drivers and shotgun guards are workers fer the stagecoaches. They expect their job to be dangerous. Passengers make for a whole lot of fuss. They'd make fer even more people talkin' to the company 'bout investigatin' the robberies."

Garrett nodded slowly. "Yeah, that makes sense. Y'know, I kinda wish Milt were here. That he hadn'ta been killed."

Jed's eyes snapped up from the flames. "Why?"

Garrett rested his elbows on his knees. "I liked him. That's all. He could always explain things to me without making me feel like I was stupid."

The next two days were spent scouting out the ambush area and getting the tree ready to set in the road. Tom assigned each of his men to their positions. Garrett was to be backup; if someone needed something, he would come out of hiding and help them. Jed was in charge of the passengers and would gather their valuables. Lefty was to help Tom take care of the driver and shotgun guard and get the strongbox. Force would only be used if it was needed.

If only they had known more about the passengers. If only...

There were a lot of "if only's" in Jed's life. If only his mother hadn't died giving him life. If only his da hadn't beaten him every chance he got. If only he hadn't gone toward the road the day he left home. If only he'd had the guts to leave the gang earlier. If only Tom would've given him any other job. If only, if only, if only!

But that was all in the past. There was no changing what was already done.

The stage was due at the ambush spot midafternoon on Tuesday. As the sun began its journey to the western horizon, they all got into position, put their masks on, and stayed hidden as they waited impatiently for the stagecoach.

It was a hot, dry afternoon. Jed was tempted to take his dark, heavy mask off and just put it back on when he saw the stage, but that would cost precious time. Putting the mask back on required tying the material behind his head to cover his whole face from the top of the nose on down. He would not have time to spare for that. They would have barely enough time as it was.

While the minutes and hours ticked slowly by, he thought back. He had no idea why he thought back, but he did. Why did he torture himself every time he was alone? Every time he waited for a robbery or a stage? Maybe to give himself an edge for the task ahead? He shook his head in confusion.

His thoughts turned to his childhood. He thought of his father, his sister, his brother. He wondered what they were doing. Were they thinking of him? Did they hate him? Did they wish against hope he would write them? Hoping he would come back?

No way! he told himself as he jerked his body into rigid attention. *There is no way I am going back there. Not till I know for sure that Da is dead, buried, and rotting in his grave.*

Jed snarled at himself. Even after his da was rotting in his grave, Jed wouldn't want to go back. His siblings were nothing to worry about. They had never done anything to stop Da, so why should he care about them and what they thought?

"Get your mind on the task," Jed reminded himself. "You are here to rob a stage. There are two passengers. You are in charge of keeping them calm and getting their money and jewelry." He drew in thick air, the dust tickling his mouth and throat as he tried to gain control. He breathed in through his nose and held his breath for a couple of seconds before letting it all out through his mouth. He repeated the exercise a few times before starting to breathe normally.

"Keep your mind on the goal," he told himself. "The box on top of the stage. That's all we need."

What about tomorrow? Won't you need more then? After the money from this robbery is gone, what will you do then? Rob another stage? Shoot another man because someone is paying you for it? Jed shook his head. If those thoughts came one more time, he knew he would end up in a crazy house. *I live for today. Tomorrow'll take care of itself. If I always worry about tomorrow, life ain't worth livin' today.*

Jed sighed and looked into the sky. The sun had begun to disappear behind the distant hills. He glanced over at where the others were waiting. Garrett stood with his back slouched against a tree, muttering silent complaints. He was ready for action, though a bit bored-looking, with his blond mustache drooping. Jed's head jerked back to look at Garrett and he scowled angrily at his maskless face. Yes, it was hot and the mask didn't help the heat a'tall, but that didn't mean he had to be stupid. There might not be time to put it back on. Jed shook his head and continued his survey.

He looked in Lefty's direction. Lefty also had his mask off, but it was in his left hand, ready to put on at a moment's notice. If he had the moment to spare. Jed's eyes narrowed as they searched for Tom. Tom always hid better than the others, so he would be harder to spot.

Ah, there he is. Behind a tree. Actually, he stood behind the tree he would let fall in the next couple of minutes. All Tom had to do was push it just right and it would fall.

Jed narrowed his eyes further. Was it just the shadows playing tricks on his eyes or was that Tom's face he saw? His whole face. Surely Tom hadn't taken his mask off, too! Jed cursed bitterly under his breath. Were they all daft? First, Tom went off the deep end and got mad about everything, then *all*, not one, but *all* of his partners were ordered to wear their masks and yet they all had taken them off. And why? Because of a little heat?

Jed cursed again. Louder this time. He didn't care if the others heard him. Maybe they'd remember to put their masks on. Did he care if they didn't? If they didn't, he could use that as an excuse for leaving and becoming a fulltime hired gun. It sure would be easier than this waiting.

He contemplated the idea and nearly jumped out of his skin when the tree hit the ground. Jed glanced at his pocket watch. *Right on time,* he thought. *The stage should be arriving any minute now.* The tree could have been dropped earlier, but Tom did not like to leave even the possibility of being caught by someone besides the stage coming up the road while the tree lay in the road.

Jed's ideas scattered as his mind went back to the task at hand. As the man with the best eyes, he was given the best position to spot the stagecoach. As soon as he saw the stage, he would give the signal and, if he caught the stage in time, his stupid partners, who still hadn't put their masks back on, would have time to fix their masks. At least he hoped they would. Muttering curses under his breath, Jed watched for the telltale dust. It would be there soon.

CHAPTER FIVE

Bump. Bump. Eat some dust. Cough. Sip water from canteen. Wait. Watch scenery. Bump some more. Trees, hills, and grass. Endless grass. Boredom. Complete and total boredom.

Joshua sighed. That about summed up his trip thus far. He tried to read, but he simply couldn't concentrate. Sitting still had always been hard for him to do. He was restless.

As he stirred and squirmed in his seat, he tried not to think about his desire for adventure. If it hadn't been for Ruth, he would have bought a horse...

I know just the one, too, he thought. *Grimm's had a beautiful stallion for sale. Black with a white, cross-like patch on his forehead. Midnight.* He closed his eyes as he dreamed.

"You're not going to sleep, are you, Joshua?" Ruth's voice broke into his thoughts.

Joshua opened his eyes as the vision of Midnight popped like a bubble. He smiled at Ruth. "No, Ruthie, I'm not. I don't see how anyone could."

Ruth wrinkled her small nose in agreement before returning her eyes to her book.

Joshua shook his head. *How could I have forgotten about Ruth?* The trip might have been able to be done faster and with less boredom without her, but where would he be without Ruth?

It had been Ruth who had pointed out his growing anger problem and where it would lead if not nipped in the bud. With Ruth's prayers and encouragement, he had been able to start controlling his anger. Now if he got angry, he usually apologized right away and made amends.

Joshua scowled at himself. *Like I did so well in the battle of wills with Matthew,* he thought. That had been the first time in a long time he had been angry with someone for three days. The worst part was that he had known right away that he was wrong and should apologize. They had both been wrong, but he knew he should have swallowed his pride earlier and apologized sooner. Yes, he had proven that he was willing to do what was needed, but it had taken much too long. He couldn't be proud of the fact that he had been the first to step forward because he had held on to the grudge.

He sighed and stared out the window. They had left the Illinois and Nebraska prairies behind and would be nearing the mountains soon. His thoughts turned to the early explorers. What would it have been like to be with Lewis and Clark, Kit Carson, or any of the other mountain men?

His mind wandered down the unbeaten paths through hostile country. He began to imagine that he had been one of the men who had struggled to survive against the elements and hostile Indians. He made friends with the Indians, he discovered new places, new adventures. He...

The stagecoach came to a sudden stop as Gage Bradford pulled the reins back. Larson's voice came low and steady, barely audible. "Stay in the stage."

Joshua could tell from his tone that something was wrong. He wanted to know what it was, but one quick look at Ruth's frightened eyes told him he needed to stay where he was. Just as he was about to move over to his sister, he heard voices behind him, at the front of the stage. *Robbers, outlaws, Indians,* he thought, alarm filling his body. *I need to keep Ruthie safe from them.* He fumbled with his army revolver as he put it in its holster, making sure his coat covered the gun.

Larson's loud voice traveled through the stagecoach roof. "What'dya want?"

The outlaws responded, but their voices were too far away to hear. Joshua's mind raced. What would happen now? Was there anything he could do to prevent these robbers? No, not with Ruth to think about. He looked over at Ruth. Ruth stared back at him, fear in her eyes. Her face lacked all color and her breathing was shallow.

"Ruth, you need to breathe."

Ruth gave a quick shake of her head as if just waking from a bad dream and started to take quick, short breaths.

The door on the driver's side rattled and Joshua lunged across to the other side of the stage to protect Ruth from whoever might put their gun through the door.

Above him, he could hear Gage and Larson arguing with the other outlaws. *Dear God, please let this not become a gunfight to the death. Protect us, Lord!* The door creaked open and a masked man stuck a pistol in the opening before bringing his head around the door.

Joshua saw a man with a black mask covering the lower half of his face. Longish red hair covered his head in a wild rat's nest. "Get out!" the man demanded in a gruff voice.

"Trust in God," Joshua hissed as he moved to step out, staring at the man in front of him. The outlaw was tall, husky, and muscular. He was a little taller than Joshua and his green eyes were slits above the mask.

The outlaw glared at Joshua while he helped Ruth out of the stagecoach. Her hand shook with slight tremors in his grasp. He gave her hand a reassuring squeeze.

The outlaw's eyes widened. "You two are nothin' but kids!"

Joshua's jaw clenched. He breathed slowly, trying to calm himself. He looked straight into the man's eyes. "I don't think that I am that much younger than you are."

The outlaw took the bait. "How old are you?"

"Seventeen," Joshua replied evenly. "You?"

"None of yer business." His focus shifted to Ruth. "Now, I need you both to do as I say and give me yer fancy stuff."

Ruth had been looking intently at the man during the whole exchange. Joshua could tell she had noticed something about him, but now was not the time to find out what. He was surprised when Ruth dared to answer his demand.

"We don't have any, Sir." Ruth's voice was just above a loud whisper and cracked.

"You really expect me to believe that, Girl?" The outlaw's eyes narrowed as he moved the business end of his pistol closer to Ruth.

Joshua stiffened. "Watch where you point that gun, Mister," he growled.

The outlaw glared at him and glanced up to the top of the stage. Joshua could hear the low rumble of voices near the horses.

The outlaw was about to say something when a gun blast echoed off the trees. The outlaw's attention jerked away from Joshua and Ruth, and Joshua took the opportunity to grab Ruth's arm and drag her around the back of the stage. He eased the other door open and grabbed their bags. Tossing them to the ground, he heard the outlaw curse before he closed the door to the stage.

He heard Ruth whispering to him, but ignored her as he climbed quietly into the stage, pulled out his knife, and cut the fabric off the seats. There had been no more gunshots and Joshua hoped that meant the first one had just been a warning shot. He bunched up the fabric and jumped out of the stage.

"Run for the woods, Ruth," he ordered. "Bring your bag with you."

Joshua breathed a quick prayer of thanks to God for giving her a trusting spirit. After they had gotten to a safe distance from the stagecoach, Joshua stopped Ruth.

"Sit down here. We might have to make an escape through the woods. I hope we won't, but we should be prepared, just in case." He handed the bundle to Ruth. "Put this in one of the bags. We'll use them as blankets if we need to camp out at all. Now, I'm going to get a little closer and watch what's going on down there. I want you to get out your paper and pencil and write down the descriptions I give you." His eyes bored into Ruth's. Her eyes were still full of fear, but there was also a glimmer of hope and determination. He allowed his expression to soften. "Pray, Ruth. Pray like you've never prayed before."

"I am," she whispered. "I have been ever since we stopped."

"Good girl," Joshua said as he turned and made his way closer to the action on the road.

CHAPTER SIX

Jed jerked his head toward the front of the stage. *Gunshots? I thought Tom didn't want this to be a murder and robbery?* He shook his head and turned back to the kids. His eyes widened as he cursed toward the empty space where they had been just seconds earlier. He slammed the stage door shut with an oath and stalked to the front of the stage where he heard a heated discussion going on.

The sight that met his eyes stunned him, if only for a second. His three partners were all standing between the felled tree and the stilled stage. They were maskless and haughty. Jed looked again. Maskless? They really had gone daft!

Jed closed his eyes, mouth stretching to a thin line under his mask. For men who said they weren't going to kill anyone, they sure were going about it the wrong way. Insulting and baiting the driver and guard would not get them to simply hand the money box over without a fight.

"Garrett!" Tom yelled. "What are you doin'? Keep that gun out of my face!"

"Sorry, Boss."

Tom turned his attention back up to the driver and guard, who were still sitting in the driver's box. With false politeness, Tom said, "Now, gentlemen, iffen you would kindly hand down the strongbox we'll let you and the passengers git on yer merry way." His smile was less than sincere.

"This money does not belong to you and never will," the driver stated, his face holding a studied and blank expression. If Jed had been a betting man, he would have bet the driver faced death every day of his life, or at the very least, didn't care one way or t'other whether he lived or not. "It is our duty to get the strongbox and the passengers safely to their destinations. If you should succeed—"

"Stop the jabberin'!" Tom ordered. His eyes flickered around and caught Jed standing nearby. "Jed. How'd it go with the passengers?"

"They didn't have any money or fancy things." Jed held his breath in for a few seconds, hoping Tom wouldn't see through his lie. No, it wasn't a lie, just hopeful thinking. Or rather, an educated guess. He doubted the kids carried anything more valuable than the boy's revolver and possibly a rifle. Yes, out West, a man could live off of just a revolver and a rifle. As long as he had ammunition, but ammunition wasn't the kind of valuable Tom was looking for.

"Fine. Point yer gun straight at the driver and be ready to shoot him if they don't listen."

"Yes, Sir." Jed did as he was told. He knew that, regardless of their cooperation, the driver and guard would be shot to avoid descriptions going out to the law. *What is Tom goin' to do about the kids?* he wondered. *Surely he won't shoot them, too? They haven't seen Tom, Lefty, and Garrett. Maybe, just maybe, Tom will let them go.*

Jed's breath exited his lungs with a whoosh as he tuned out Tom's demands and threats. This outlaw business had been getting on his nerves for some time now. He needed something new to do. Maybe he could convince Tom to let him go.

Jed shook his head. Sometime ago, he had been proud that he was Tom's right-hand man—that he had the best work ethic, did what Tom asked without question, was the best shot—but now he knew there was no way Tom would simply let him go.

Tom's voice cut into his thoughts. "You give us that thar strongbox or we'll bring the passengers out and shoot 'em!"

Jed flinched at Tom's words. "Tom," he protested, "they're just kids."

"You getting a conscience, Jed?" Tom glared at him before turning his attention back to the driver.

The driver stared into the space above Tom's head and said nothing. His hands rested on his thighs, the reins held taut, despite the slight fidgeting of the horses. Tom sneered as he walked toward Jed. "We'll get the kids then."

Jed stared at Tom, eyes narrowed, then turned around and headed for the door of the stage.

When he got to the door, he stopped and turned to Tom. "Tom, the kids are gone. They bolted when you shot off your gun."

Tom stared at Jed. "And you let them?"

"I was too surprised by the gun going off. I let my attention slip from them."

Tom cursed loudly.

"They were s'pose ta convince those two..." His thought trailed off as another gunshot echoed off the hills. Tom and Jed stared at each other for a minute before they rushed to the front of the stage.

The first sight to meet Jed's eyes was Garrett writhing on the ground, clutching his arm. Lefty stared at Garrett, but something must have caught his attention from the corner of his eye, because he lifted his rifle to his shoulder and shot the guard.

Jed glanced up at the guard as Lefty shot him. The guard had taken advantage of the distraction from what, or rather whoever, had shot Garrett. From the position of the guard's rifle, the guard had not shot Garrett.

"What in blazes is goin' on?" Tom demanded.

"Somebody's in the woods shootin' at us!" Garrett shouted, pain lacing his every word.

Tom darted out of the path of the jumpy horses. Gunshots and horses did not mix well. Blood and horses didn't mix well either. Horses feared the smell of blood and often went wild. Lefty staggered backwards, trying to stay out of reach of the horses' hooves. Jed moved away from the stage, but kept the stage between himself and the woods and stayed close enough to the carriage to have a clean shot at the driver without the driver being able to shoot him.

The guard's body slumped against the driver, the rifle butt leaning against the driver's leg. Using his knees to hold the reins just tight enough to keep the horses steady, but just loose enough to give them some freedom, the driver grabbed the rifle and shot Lefty through the heart before Jed knew what his plan was.

Jed's pistol was already in his hand and he shot the driver through the head just as he saw Tom fall to the ground, a dark patch growing on his leg. The driver's knees instinctively slackened as his body slumped forward. The horses became even more nervous as the reins slackened. Jed stayed behind the wheel of the stage, keeping low to the ground and talking in a quiet, soothing voice to the horses.

As he waited to see what would happen with whoever was in the woods, he used the time and the silence to think. Most likely, it was the kids in the woods. He wondered briefly if it might be Indians, but dismissed the thought. *I should've taken the guns away from 'em. They must have somehow known that flight was their best option. Not good news for us.* He glanced at the injured men. Of course, from the looks of the wounds his partners had, Jed wondered if the gang would even exist in a few more days.

Jed wracked his brain for options. He had to get Tom and Garrett out of the road, but he couldn't do that until he was sure the kids were gone.

"Tom," he hissed. Tom turned his head toward Jed. "I'm goin' to the woods to see if the kids are still around. I'll be right back."

Tom blinked his eyes in a slow motion. Jed looked at Tom's leg and saw that his pant leg was already full of blood. "See if you can slow some of that bleeding. I'll be as fast as I can."

Jed stood up slowly and went around to the back of the stagecoach. He looked in the direction of where the kids had to have been. He didn't see anything, but from what he had noticed, he didn't think the kids would have been stupid enough to be in plain sight. He ran to the woods and darted from tree to tree.

It took him just over a minute to find where the boy had made his stand. The pine needles and leaves were matted down and a wayward spent shell lay next to a tree. He was long gone which meant his sister was, too. Nodding to himself, he looked around, carefully noticing the layout of the trees and any other identifying marks. If there was one thing he could predict, it was Tom's next order to him: Follow the kids and kill 'em.

After another quick glance around him, Jed hurried back to the two injured men.

Cursing to himself, Jed wrapped Tom's handkerchief around his wounded leg. "That kid is good with a gun," Tom hissed through his teeth. "He got me right in the worst place."

"He could've just been lucky," Jed said.

Tom swore as Jed tightened the kerchief. "I don't think so, Jed."

Jed moved over to help Garrett, but found him already taking care of himself. He had used his teeth and good hand to tighten his kerchief around his wound. By the time Jed was done with Tom, Garrett had started dragging Lefty's body off the road and into the woods. Jed hurried into the woods and began digging a shallow grave with a sharp, flat rock and his hands.

After finishing the grave, he returned to the stage and dragged the two bodies off the driver's box and slung them across his shoulders. He started toward the grave and caught Garrett's curious gaze on him.

"What?" Jed demanded.

"Just leave 'em to the buzzards, Jed," Garrett said. "It ain't worth the time to bury 'em."

"It'll only take a minute if you'll let me do my work," Jed countered as he continued on to the grave and dumped them in with Lefty's body. Knowing he had little time and that Garrett and Tom were losing patience with him, he hurriedly covered them with dirt, leaves, and the few rocks and dead limbs he could find.

By the time he finished this task, Garrett had climbed into the driver's box and held on to the reins, a pained expression on his face.

Jed looked toward Tom. He still lay on the ground in front of the horses and had just regained consciousness.

"Jed," Tom called.

Jed walked over to him. "Yeah, Boss?"

"Git me in the stage." His breathing grew ragged and labored.

"Are you crazy, Tom?" Jed exclaimed. "The stage'll be too easy to keep track of. We need to ditch the stage. You'll have to ride one of the horses."

Tom's glazed eyes stared back at Jed with a mixture of horror and pain.

Jed sighed. "I know it won't be pleasant, but Garrett'll take care of you."

Tom closed his eyes in resignation and nodded. "Fine, just git after them kids. They can't git ta town."

Jed put his hand on Tom's arm. "I'll do it," he said. "You just worry 'bout gettin' better. I'll meet you at the hideout in a few days."

Tom grimaced. "I know y'all do it and do it well."

Jed lifted Tom onto one of the horses.

"Garrett, get him back to the hideout and keep his wound clean. You'll have to ride double so Tom don't fall off."

"Will do. You just worry 'bout them kids."

"I'll get 'em." Jed narrowed his eyes. "I'll get 'em if it's the last thing I do."

Jed heaved the tree out of the way while Garret got off the stage and moved next to the horse. Once the tree lay alongside the road, Garrett swung into the saddle behind Tom. Jed watched them go before heading in the direction the gunshots had come from.

At least the kids let me know where they were by shooting that gun off, he thought. Although that thought was little comfort since they had injured two of his gang members. Jed scanned the road to make sure all evidence of the robbery was gone.

Once he was reassured, he plunged into the woods to go after the two kids. Hopefully in a couple of more hours, he would be on his way to the hideout and some warm food and coffee. Not to mention a little richer and having killed two more people. Two kids.

He shuddered before forcibly blocking the thought out of his head. *They've seen too much. They're practically adults anyway. If they live on, they'll just become law-abidin' citizens who condemn outlaws and everythin' we stand for. Not to mention that the boy could eventually become the law somewheres.*

A crumpled bunch of grass, leaves, and moss caught his attention and he examined it. A cruel smile covered his face. He was on the right trail already.

CHAPTER SEVEN

Once safe in the woods, Joshua rapidly scanned the scene by the stagecoach. Four bad guys, two good guys. Bradford and Larson were still in the driver's box. The guard cradled his rifle. Three of the outlaws stood in a row in front of the horses, each holding his gun, ready to shoot. The only masked outlaw stood to the side, his pistol pointed at Bradford.

Joshua glanced behind him. "Ruth?"

"Ready." Her voice was quiet and quavered.

Joshua took a deep breath and listened to the angry discussion for a minute.

"You give us that thar strongbox or we'll bring the passengers out and shoot 'em!" the leader threatened.

"Tom," the man in the mask said, "they're just kids. Don't use them."

"You getting a conscience, Jed?" Tom glared at him before turning his attention back to the driver.

Joshua tuned their shouts out. "Okay, Ruth, write this down. Tom: the leader; probably just over six foot, dark, short hair with a gruff, angry voice. In his early to mid-thirties. Jed: six foot four, stocky and muscular, seems to be second-in-command and the smartest of the group. Roughly twenty. Wearing a mask, some red hair shows through. Probably has a beard. The other two are under six foot. One has dark blond or light brown hair and is stocky and cocky. The other is swarthy, reddish-brown hair, and muscular. Both are probably in their mid- to late twenties." He paused. "Got it all, Ruth?"

"Yes." Her response was stronger this time. Joshua breathed a sigh of relief.

Joshua watched the scene below for a few more seconds and was about to turn away when he noticed Tom and Jed split off to the side of the stage while the other two pointed their guns at the driver and guard.

"Oh, God, no! They wouldn't!"

"What?" Ruth exclaimed.

"Stay back!" Joshua ordered. He kept his eyes on the scene below while waving his arm in Ruth's direction. "Get deeper into the woods and stay down low to the ground."

Joshua hazarded a glance behind him. He could no longer see Ruth and sighed in relief. In one swift move, he grabbed his rifle and lay flat to the ground. Extending the rifle, he aimed at the shorter man whose gun was pointed at Bradford. Perspiration gathered on Joshua's forehead and his breathing became ragged. *The shoulder. I can't kill the man, just aim for the shoulder.* Joshua took a deep breath and let it out slowly. Just as the outlaw was about to shoot, Joshua's bullet hit the man in the left shoulder. The outlaw's rifle dropped to the ground.

His partner glanced in Joshua's direction before calmly killing the shotgun guard. During the commotion, Mr. Bradford grabbed the guard's rifle and shot the blond man with it. Tom and Jed ran around to the front of the stage.

"What in blazes is goin' on?" Tom demanded.

"Somebody's in the woods shootin' at us!" the short outlaw said through gritted teeth.

Tom swore and aimed his gun at the driver, who hopelessly tried to reload the rifle. In a vain attempt to give Bradford a fighting chance, Joshua clenched his jaw and shot Tom. He felt a little sick about crippling the man, outlaw though he was.

As he levered another bullet into his rifle barrel, he saw Jed bring his pistol up and watched helplessly as Jed shot the driver.

Joshua had no time for regrets. His heart in his throat and nausea rolling through his body, he picked up as many spent shells as he could find before he belly-crawled deeper into the woods, found Ruth, and they began their escape.

They ran blindly for a few minutes before Joshua stopped to get his bearings.

"We're headed the wrong direction." Joshua breathed deeply. "We need to go at a slower pace and with more care so Jed can't track us."

Ruth's eyes went wide with terror. "Why would he follow us?"

"One of his buddies is dead, another almost dead, and the other is badly injured." He stopped as he thought the events through. "I think Tom and Jed were on their way to kill us when the gunfight started."

Ruth's mouth opened in shock. "Why?" she whispered. "Why would they do that?"

Joshua set his lips in a grim line. "We are witnesses. We know what they look like and what they did. They can't let us live or we will give a lawman their descriptions. My guess is that so far, they have stayed off of the wanted posters; they can't let that change now."

Ruth nodded. "Let's move." Her wide brown eyes spoke volumes. Despite her fear and confusion, she trusted God and her brother to keep her safe. Joshua could only hope and pray that he could do so.

"God will keep us safe." Joshua tried to smile reassuringly as he led her along on their way to safety.

They trudged through the dense underbrush, being careful where they stepped. Joshua could only guess at how good Jed was at tracking. He chose to err on the side of caution. Joshua kept his eyes darting ahead, searching for the best paths. He glanced back at Ruth and saw her holding her skirts up to keep them away from the brush. He smiled encouragement to her but did not speak. Although it seemed like they were going slow, because of the hills, his breathing had already become difficult.

Joshua stopped at the top of another short hill to catch his breath, let Ruth catch up, and study the terrain.

"How much further are we going today?" Ruth asked as she joined him. She wheezed and Joshua mentally chided himself for having pushed her so hard.

Joshua took a deep breath and looked around again. "I was hoping to get to those rocks before dark."

Ruth looked at the outcropping in the distance. "A couple more miles, then?"

Joshua looked at her intently. "Can you make it?"

Ruth took a deep breath, looked at the rocks, squared her shoulders, and looked into his eyes. "If it means safety for the night, I can make it."

Joshua grinned. *That's my darling, sweet sister. Give her a goal and a time limit and she will do her*

best to reach it. *Regardless of how hard it may be.*
"Let's go," Joshua said. "We'll make it and with time to spare."

Stepping carefully, they worked their way through the dense brush.

There were no clouds in the sky and the moon shone bright around Joshua and Ruth as they prepared a camp in the rocks. Joshua gathered some dry leaves and sticks while Ruth prepared two beds of pine boughs. Once the beds were made, Ruth left the area of the camp and wrote in her diary while Joshua made the final preparations.

He took the flint and steel out of his pocket and started the leaves on fire, putting two small pieces of wood on top when the sticks had lit. Looking out over the woods from which they had just come, Joshua prayed, "God, if Jed is watching us right now, please let him be fooled into thinking we are staying here."

Joshua knelt beside the fake bed for Ruth and tucked the blanket around the log. Something rustled in the brush next to him. He froze, fear gripping his entire body. Had Jed found them already and come in for the kill? After a terrifying few seconds, his body caught up to his brain and he flattened himself onto the ground, waited another couple of seconds, then with slow, deliberate movements, belly-crawled into the shadows until he had gone far enough away from the fire to avoid being seen.

Heart still pounding like a drum beating a hasty retreat, he rejoined his sister. "The camp is ready." He swallowed hard, trying to moisten his dry throat.

Ruth didn't respond immediately, finishing her sentence. "I'm done writing now."

Joshua glanced around with nervous movements as she finished writing. He wanted to get out of there, but he also didn't want to frighten Ruth. He nodded. "Ready now?"

Ruth smiled up at him as she lifted her arm. He took her hand and pulled her up. "I know this will fool him. We need to do this if we are going to have a fighting chance."

Joshua searched her face as her calm expression soothed his rattled nerves. *Thank You, God, for giving me such a plucky little sister.* "After you, M'lady," he said with a bow.

Ruth slapped a hand to her mouth to stop the giggle as she stepped forward and led the way off the rocks. They traveled in the moonlit night until Ruth could go no farther. Joshua made a pine bough bed for Ruth but lit no fire here. He knew they could not risk being seen this time. He prayed that it would not get too cold at night. October weather could be unpredictable in Illinois, but he had no idea what it was like in Wyoming.

Ruth was asleep almost as soon as she lay down, but Joshua's mind kept him awake. Knowing Jed must be near, he couldn't help but worry. As he waited for the dawn, he prayed for God's protection and thanked Him for his Indian friend in Illinois who had taught him so many valuable survival skills.

Sleep continued to be elusive until an hour before the sun began to creep above the distant hills. Joshua's eyelids drooped and he finally gave in and fell into a fitful slumber.

CHAPTER EIGHT

The gang was down to three if Tom lived. Jed knew that the chances of Tom recovering from his wound were slim. Tom'd been right. The bullet had gone into the main blood vessel in his leg. He had lost a lot of blood by the time Jed had gotten to him. After losing so much blood, there wasn't much a body could do, even if one was a doctor.

'Course, since they were outlaws and had to keep a low profile, they didn't get a doctor's help. Ever. Especially right after a robbery.

Jed shook the cobwebs and thoughts out of his head. He had a mission to accomplish. Maybe by the time he was done, Tom would be dead and, as former second-in-command, he could break up the gang and send Garrett to do something else. Anything else.

Jed set the thoughts aside and headed into the woods after the kids. They had hurt his friends and he wouldn't let them get away with it. They only had about a half-hour head start on him and were sure to go slower. Especially since the girl had skirts to fight with. *I should be able to catch 'em within a coupla hours.*

The trail was easy to follow for a while. Jed trudged along their wide, trampled trail. Along the way, he saw small bits of brown calico sticking to the surrounding underbrush.

After a mad dash to get away, the kids started getting smart. They slowed down, changed direction, and took more care in where they put their feet down. Jed grunted in frustration as the trail started to get harder to follow. Maybe it would take the rest of the day instead of just a couple hours.

Another hour passed. Jed started muttering to himself. "Are they part Injun? This trail is almost impossible to follow." He narrowed his eyes, his face becoming a hard scowl. He glanced up at the sky. The sun would be setting in a few hours. He had to catch them before it did.

He kept his eyes sharp on the faint trail. Even the bits of material had disappeared. He wondered how they had managed that, but dismissed the thought.

As he continued on after the kids, he thought about a life without the gang. Could he actually do it? He stopped walking. With Tom on his deathbed, he could leave without any worry about Tom coming after him.

Jed continued walking. He looked around him. What he wouldn't give for Milton to be there. Or even Ty or Carson. As clueless as they had been about being outlaws, they had at least been pleasant to be around. Jed clenched his jaw and gritted his teeth.

So many dead. So many lives wasted. What would they have been if they hadn't become outlaws? Milton might've become a schoolteacher. He probably would've even made a good one. Ty and Carson? Too bad court jesters were a thing of the past. They would have made a great pair of jesters.

Lefty. If he'd have put his fast gun hand and quick thinking to good use, he could have been a sheriff. Garrett? He definitely should've been a blacksmith. He had the build, muscle, and know-how for it. Now Tom was a harder one to figure out.

Jed squinted at the trail and looked around to study the land around him. The terrain was getting rockier. He swore. He'd always had trouble tracking on rocky ground. What was he doing, anyway? Who had the kids seen? One of the men they'd seen was dead, another nearly dead. He'd been wearing a mask. No, the mask hadn't covered up all of his distinctive red hair, but it covered enough.

The only other man they'd seen was Garrett and he didn't have any features that would stand out too much. Why go after the kids at all?

Jed narrowed his eyes at the rock face ahead without seeing it. Oh yes, that was why. They had killed one of his friends, his boss was as good as dead, and Garrett was hurt bad. If he didn't avenge his friends' deaths what was the point of having friends? Most especially when those friends were more like family than his real family.

Jed squared his shoulders and trudged on for another half hour. *There has to be a better way!* His thoughts turned bitter. He looked around him. *That rock outcropping would be a good place for them to stop. I'll watch it from a distance. When they light a fire, I'll sneak into the camp and grab the girl. The boy'll have to come with me then.*

His near silent laugh sounded cruel, even to his own ears. When had he become like this? He shook the dismal thoughts from his mind.

He inched his way through the woods, watching the faint trail with a shrewd and practiced eye, all while keeping a close eye on the rock outcropping. He reached the edge of the woods and stopped. The outcropping was a short half-hour hike uphill. He would stop here for now and just wait and watch.

The moon lit up the area, but it wouldn't be for long. Jed's eyes flickered in a nervous reaction to the darkening sky. The cloudless sky showed most of the stars and the moon would set in another hour or so. His heavy eyelids drooped shut. With a shake of his head, Jed blinked his eyes several times as he focused his vision back to the rocks. The flicker of a flame caused him to blink rapidly and widen his eyes. He stifled a yell of triumph. They had started a fire! He was now wide awake, sleepiness all but forgotten.

A shadow moved around the camp. Since he saw no skirts, he could only assume it was the boy. He grinned in evil delight. After trailing the kids this far, he had thought they would be smart enough not to start a fire, particularly in a place where the light would reflect so well.

Jed chuckled to himself and shook his head. His chuckle died as he saw the boy tuck his sister in and lay down near her. Jed waited with a patience bred from experience. He wanted to give them time to fall asleep so he could take them by surprise.

His feet followed a natural, smooth trail around the rocks, keeping his approach silent. He scanned the area lit up by the fire. Seeing nothing amiss, he crept up to where the girl was sleeping. He grabbed the girl and pointed his pistol at the boy.

Just as his mouth opened to tell the boy to surrender, he realized that something was wrong. All he held was an empty blanket.

"Aaauuugghh!" His yell of frustration bounced off the rocks many times, echoing back and forth.

How could I have been so stupid to think that they would just give themselves up like this? he berated himself. *I should have known they would do something like this. But no, I had to think that they would make a simple, stupid mistake.*

Jed fumed as he watched the flames of the fire flicker against the rocks. He sat down on the bed the boy was supposed to be in. He looked down at the bed in surprise. It was actually almost soft. Considering the bed was on a foundation of stone, it was very soft. He lifted the blanket. Pine branches and a blanket. That's all it was.

He stood up swiftly as his eyes started drooping. Searching, he thought he could see a faint trail. He followed it down the rock. Darkness surrounded him. He looked up at the sky. No moon. Then he remembered seeing the moon setting. *My brain is so tired it can't even remember something as simple as the moon setting.*

His eyelids felt heavy. He shook his head. *May's well go back to the camp they made. I can't go any further tonight anyway. No point in it going to waste.* He turned around and headed back to the fire. The camp would be a good lesson to him in the morning, too. He would need to remember to never underestimate this boy and his quick mind. His eyes narrowed. When he found them, he would make them wish they had never been born.

CHAPTER NINE

Joshua woke up as the sun started breaking over the eastern horizon. He rubbed his eyes, trying to wake up completely. *Thank You, Lord, for keeping us safe last night.* He pushed his sore body out of the bed of pine and slowly stretched. *And help me stay awake and alert today.* After less than two hours of restless sleep, he should not be this sore. Then he remembered why. He wasn't used to the rigors of hiking for a whole day.

As Ruth continued to sleep, he scouted around for something to eat. After a quick search, he found a small, edible root and returned to camp.

By the time he got back, Ruth had started packing what little they had.

"I found some food. It's not much, but at least we will have something to eat."

Ruth nodded. She was being too quiet. No "Good morning," or "What did you find?" Concerned, Joshua watched her for a few seconds. "What's wrong, Ruth?"

Ruth shook her head, still not saying anything. Joshua stepped in front of her, grabbed her left shoulder, and lifted her chin. "What is it?"

"Nothing," she whispered.

"Yes, there is. Something is wrong. You can't convince me otherwise." He noticed that she wasn't even looking him in the eye. She always looked him in the eye.

Tears sprang to her eyes. "I'm just not used to this. You know I don't handle these types of situations very well. Now we are out here in the middle of who-knows-where with practically no food and we're being chased by a madman who wants to kill us. I'm sore, I didn't sleep well, I'm hungry, and thirsty. I don't do well on wilderness trips, Joshua. You've dragged me on enough of them to know that. And any time I think about Mr. Bradford and Mr. Larson, it hurts so bad, I can hardly breathe." Ruth started sobbing into his shirt.

Joshua's heart tightened. He didn't know how much farther they needed to go and Ruth had already started getting discouraged. "Oh, Ruth. I'm so sorry. I know you don't handle wilderness trips well. I don't know why God is allowing this to happen, but we need to trust that He knows what He is doing. I need you to stand strong for me. This isn't going to be easy for either of us, especially if we don't find a town soon. I know you don't like this." He searched his brain for something, anything, useful. What should he tell his sister? How could he convince her to continue?

"Remember Pa's favorite verses?" he asked. "'Moreover, brethren, I declare unto you the gospel which I preached unto you, which also ye have received, and wherein ye stand; By which also ye are saved, if ye keep in memory what I preached unto you, unless ye have believed in vain.'" He pulled her close and wrapped his arms around her. "Stand strong on God's promises. You can make it through this, Ruth. I have faith that God can get you and me through this."

Ruth's head leaned into his chest as she cried. He held her tight until her sobs started to slow. "You did well yesterday, Ruth. You can do it again. With God's help, we can both do this. I'm having a hard time, too. I promised everybody I would take care of you."

He held Ruth out at arm's length and looked into her eyes. His throat felt tight. "Then this happens. I thought protecting you would be easy. All I had to do was make sure nobody tried to steal you from me or look at you wrong. I didn't think it would be like this. Now I need to protect you from wild animals, keep you alive, stay ahead of a murderous outlaw, feed you somehow in the wilderness without being able to have a fire and without killing anything for fear of Jed hearing the gun."

Joshua let go of Ruth, his arms dropped to his sides, and he looked away from her. He was already overwhelmed and he had yet to figure out what the best route for the day would be. "I feel as lost as you do, Ruth. Together we can pull through this or die trying."

Ruth gazed into her brother's deep brown eyes, fear etched into her own. Her eyes softened as she struggled to control her emotions. She swallowed hard. "Yes, we can do this," she said, her voice stronger than it had been earlier. She straightened her shoulders and clenched her jaw in determination.

The corners of Joshua's mouth curved upward in a weak smile. "Good. Let's get moving before Jed finds us." Oh, how he loved his sister. Once she put her mind on something, nothing could stop her. Sometimes it took a little nudging, but she would do it anyway.

They covered a lot of ground until midmorning when Joshua found a stream and they made a quick stop. The water from the stream was the first water they had found since the previous night.

"This water tastes good!" Joshua exclaimed.

"I think just about anything would taste good right now," Ruth laughed.

Joshua nodded in mock seriousness. "True."

At noon, they climbed a steep hill overlooking the valley they had been traveling in the last couple of hours. Joshua stopped and turned to have a look around the valley.

"He's still behind us."

"Good," Ruth replied. "We need to keep it that way."

"Right. Here, let's divide this root I found. We can eat while we walk."

The moon was bright again that night, but neither Joshua nor Ruth noticed. As soon as they lay down on the ground they were fast asleep. Tonight, Joshua didn't even think about keeping awake. He needed his strength for the next day. Even so, he did his best to keep an ear out for noises. As he drifted to sleep, he thanked God for making him a light sleeper.

In the morning, Joshua and Ruth scouted around for more edible plants. They were each able to find a few and decided to eat half of them right away.

"Tonight, I'm going to see about getting us some meat. Jed or no Jed, we need some substantial food. Then we'll find a good hiding place to build a small fire to roast the meat over."

Ruth groaned. "That sounds so good, but don't talk about it right now, please."

Joshua grimaced. "Sorry. You're right, as usual."

Ruth stuck her tongue out at Joshua and he burst out laughing. "You haven't done that in a while. I thought you were too grown up for that."

"Being hot, dirty, tired, and hungry brings out the worst in people," Ruth retorted.

Joshua grinned at her. "True. Very true."

They found another stream late in the morning and it brightened their spirits. Ruth began humming her favorite hymn, "A Mighty Fortress Is Our God." Joshua joined her humming, knowing that singing it out loud would be too risky. He found the words from verse two to be encouraging:

> *Did we in our own strength confide,*
> *Our striving would be losing;*
> *Were not the right Man on our side,*
> *The Man of God's own choosing...*

At noon they found another stream and a little food.

"We need to throw Jed off," Joshua said, staring into the water. He tried not to think about how many hills they had climbed up and down. So far, his goal had been to head northwest in the general direction of Montana. He debated within himself on whether to change his plans.

Ruth cocked her head to the side and interrupted his thoughts. "How?"

"We'll walk in the stream going east instead of west. That way he can't track us and we can put some more distance between us. Hopefully he won't guess which direction we really went."

Ruth nodded and stepped into the stream. "Which way, Brother Dear?"

Joshua pointed, a smile playing at his mouth as Ruth started wading through the stream. He was quick to join her.

They walked in the stream for a half hour before climbing onto the bank. Joshua's mood started to darken as they trudged farther on. They had still seen no sign of civilization. Or much of anything except trees and rocks for that matter. The hills kept getting steeper and bushier. Ruth struggled to keep up and her skirts kept snagging on the bushes.

Joshua could tell that Ruth was getting tired and discouraged. He tried to quote Scripture, but he couldn't think of anything. He gave up the attempt.

Stopping at the top of another hill, he heard Ruth muttering as she climbed up behind him.

"The Lord is my shepherd, I shall not want. He leadeth me beside still waters." She stopped when she reached the top. "Can we sit for a few minutes?" She breathed hard. Joshua was too exhausted to talk. He nodded and collapsed next to her.

Once they had both caught their breath, Joshua asked, "Can you finish quoting the Psalm?"

"Only if you finish it with me," she replied with a smile just visible in her eyes.

"'The Lord is my shepherd; I shall not want. He maketh me to lie down in green pastures: he leadeth me beside the still waters. He restoreth my soul: he leadeth me in the paths of righteousness for his name's sake.

"'Yea, though I walk through the valley of the shadow of death, I will fear no evil: for thou art with me; thy rod and thy staff they comfort me. Thou preparest a table before me in the presence of mine enemies: thou anointest my head with oil; my cup runneth over. Surely goodness and mercy shall follow me all the days of my life: and I will dwell in the house of the Lord for ever.'"

Joshua sighed. "I love that Psalm!"

"So do I."

Joshua jumped up suddenly. "We need to get moving before I can't get myself to move from here." He held his hand out and Ruth grabbed it, pulling herself up off the ground.

Late that afternoon, Joshua saw a deer and decided they needed food badly enough to risk Jed hearing the shot. He abandoned his snare idea and crept closer and took a clean shot at the deer. They would have fresh meat tonight for supper.

Ruth was grinning when he came back to her with the deer slung across his shoulders. "We get a feast tonight." She held out her hands.

Joshua stared at the greens she held and his face broke into a broad smile. "We certainly will."

They built a fire in a small hollow and roasted as much of the meat as they could. The deer was big enough to feed them for a long time if it would last, but Joshua knew it wouldn't last and they would have to leave much of the meat behind. He hated wasting the food, but he couldn't do anything about it. As it was, they would have a hard enough time carrying the meat they were keeping. They had been forced to put the meat in the carpet bag and leave their change of clothes behind.

Joshua breathed a sigh of relief after feeling full for the first time in days. *God, help us find a town soon. We can't make it much longer.*

CHAPTER TEN

Jed squinted as the sun started to light up the sky. He had been up for almost an hour already and was ready to get back on the trail, but had been forced to wait for the sun so he could see the trail. The problem with waiting for the sun was that there was too much time to think. And too much time for his stomach to complain.

"How have those kids survived this long?" he asked himself. He glared up at the rocks surrounding him. "They can't have much food. If they've got any a'tall. Now, me? I'm used to goin' without for a few days." He scoffed. "I doubt them kids are. They've gotta be at least as tired and hungry as me. More so."

He gave a halfhearted, less than humorous chuckle. *Of course,* he thought, *they also have each other to keep company with. I don't have no one to keep me company. Just me and my dreary thoughts.*

The sun climbed over the hill and light spilled onto the trail. Jed leaped up, doused the fire, and got started down the trail. He followed the faint trail for half a day before the rumbling in his stomach got to him.

"I've gotta get me somethin' to eat soon," he mumbled. He looked around the woods, but saw nothing. He could probably make it another day, but he wouldn't be in even close to top condition. His tracking would suffer, not to mention his aim and judgment. And then there was always his temper. When he was starving, his anger erupted faster than when he had eaten something.

As if in answer to his thoughts, Jed heard a rustle nearby and turned his head toward it, his rifle automatically moving into position. A rabbit hopped across the path a few feet in front of him and Jed took a clean shot at it. The rabbit's momentum took it off the path and Jed hurried after it into the brush.

As he picked up the rabbit, his ears perked at the sound of running water. He closed his eyes and listened to the water. It was music to his ears. *After all these hours today, there is finally some more water. Why, oh why didn't I take one of our canteens?*

His practical side responded again. *You know exactly why. You were thinking you would only be gone a few hours, not a few days.* Jed scowled as he neared the stream. Yep, that was exactly why he hadn't brought a canteen.

Huffing in frustration, Jed trudged to the stream and washed the blood off the rabbit before tying it to his game belt. Once that was taken care of, he knelt down and drank some of the cool, refreshing water.

He let a mouthful of water stand in his mouth for a few minutes while he looked around. The bank opposite him wasn't very far away and he squinted his eyes, confused. As far as he could tell, there were no tracks. *Maybe they somehow hid the tracks?* He crossed the stream, reaching the opposite bank in three large strides.

Standing on the edge of the stream, he stared at the bank in disbelief. Nothing. No tracks, no sign of covered-up tracks. He turned around and looked up and down the stream. It ran from east to west.

Common sense told him they would've headed west for two reasons. Number one, their general direction so far had pointed to the west. Secondly, heading west would mean following the stream with the current instead of against it. Walking against the current was hard at any time, but in skirts it would be even worse. The current didn't seem to be strong, but it would be strong enough, and cold enough, to possibly become a problem.

But what does that matter? Jed criticized himself. He should be trying to figure out what they were doing. If they did decide to walk in the stream, why would they go out of their way?

111

To throw you off, Jed, the antagonist in him whispered. Jed pondered the thought. Would they try to throw him off like that? After all, they had made a fake camp that first night. Maybe this was just another trick.

But the girl is wearing heavy skirts, the water is cold, and they would be heading in the opposite direction. Surely they wouldn't intentionally make this harder on themselves.

Jed turned west. If he didn't find them by the end of the day he would make a fire, roast his rabbit, and get some sleep. He could figure out what to do in the morning.

The sun had almost set before Jed found a good place for camp. There had yet to be any sign of the kids leaving the stream and, despite the difficulties involved, Jed had begun to think they had to have gone upstream.

Jed pulled out his flint and stone and lit a small fire for roasting his rabbit. He was ravenous and ate everything but the one leg he would save for the next day.

If I don't find 'em or their trail by the end of tomorrow, I may's well head into Rock Springs. I won't catch 'em if I don't hit on their trail again. He narrowed his eyes into slits. "I can always find 'em some other way. And I will."

A sudden thought darted into his mind. What would people think if they saw him talking to himself? Then again, what did it matter? No one was around to see him or hear him.

"And sometimes, it's nice to hear a human voice, even if it is just mine. After bein' completely alone almost three days, I'm ready for some human company." His short laugh was almost bitter. "Even the kids would be welcome company."

Except that you have to kill them when you find them, an inner voice taunted him.

Jed scowled. "Right. I suppose I do. Well, once I find 'em, I'll head to Rock Springs or wherever the closest town is. There'll be plenty of humans there."

Jed stared into the fire. He wondered if the kids even knew they were so close to a town. *Probably not,* he thought. They didn't seem to be heading anywhere in the right direction.

Stealing the idea the boy had given him, Jed found some pine branches and made a bed out of them. He put another piece of wood on the fire and lay back on the branches. *Now for some sleep,* Jed thought as he closed his eyes and listened to the crickets and night birds singing their haunting melodies.

The next morning, Jed followed the stream back to where he had started the day before. Investigating the shore closely, he decided there was little chance of finding any sign there and headed east. After twenty minutes of steady walking, he still hadn't come across the trail.

He stopped, looking all around him. Those kids had him confused and baffled. Where could they have gone?!? It hardly seemed possible that they would have walked upstream in that cold water for more than a half hour. His feet were going numb just thinking about it.

Well, there's nothin' I can do but head northwest and see if I can't come across their trail somewhere else. They already have at least a half day's start on me. I'll be lucky if I catch 'em now.

The scowl was starting to become a permanent fixture on his face. Almost as permanent as his nose. *I should just give up. I'll never catch 'em.*

Sure you will. Jest head northwest, find a town, and ask about 'em there.

Yeah. Like no one will get suspicious 'bout me? And by then my face'll be plastered on wanted posters everywhere.

No it won't. You were the only smart one and you wore a mask. They have no idea what your face looks like.

Jed jerked his head up from his contemplation of the grass beneath his feet. "That's right. They don't have a proper description of me without my face. They don't know for sure if my nose is small or large. They couldn't know if I have any facial hair or how long my hair really is."

His hand went instinctively up to his shoulder-length red hair. "They might know the color... But lots of people have red hair," he reasoned with himself. "And lots of them are my height and build. They can't put me on a wanted poster that easy!"

Jed lifted his head up and walked on toward the northwest. At the end of the day, he was exhausted, hot, hungry, and thirsty. Again. He found a small pond and drank some of the tepid water. Not very refreshing, but it would have to do. He pulled out the rabbit leg and took slow, deliberate bites as he walked on through the gathering darkness.

If his memory served him correctly, Rock Springs ought to be nearby. Maybe he could hear something about the kids. If not, he could at least find some sort of job to do until he could hire out as a gunfighter.

Jed trudged through the moonlit night, determined to get close to town before dark. He mounted one last hill and saw lights in the windows of the houses. In the morning, he would go down the hill and see what he could find out.

Even if he didn't hear anything about the kids, he would just keep on moving what he hoped was the direction the kids had been traveling. He would find those kids. If for nothing else, simply because they had killed one of his friends and injured two others. He wouldn't think about the fact that they had also ruined the life he had known for the past seven years.

Before, his goal had been whatever Tom decided to do next. Now, he had a new one: find those kids. Even if it was the last thing he did on this earth.

CHAPTER ELEVEN

They had left the stagecoach four days earlier and there was still no town to be found. Joshua had known there weren't many towns out West, but he hadn't thought it would be this bad. They should have at least come across a road, a path, or a lone house. But they hadn't even seen the smoke of a chimney or campfire anywhere.

Another long, tedious day passed. They started rationing their meat and stopped talking to each other unless it was necessary. They knew that if they did talk, they would probably end up saying a lot of things they would regret later.

Their conversations consisted of "Let's take a breather"; "I hear a stream over there"; "Let's stop here for the night"; "Can you get the firewood tonight?" Occasionally one of them would pray out loud, quote Bible verses, or start singing. Otherwise, they walked on in silence, tired from lack of sleep on hard ground, lack of food, lack of water, and lack of hope. Tired of smelling themselves and each other. Tired of walking.

That night, Joshua took longer than usual finding wood for the fire. When he got back, he found Ruth crying.

The wood he carried fell to the ground and he rushed over to her. "What's wrong?"

"I don't know!" she sobbed. "I just felt like crying. I want to go home!" Her words fell from her mouth like a pianist with faulty rhythm.

Joshua put his arms around her and rocked back and forth. "We'll get out of this soon," he whispered in her ear. "There has to be a town nearby. I just know there has to be." *God, let it be so. Ruth is too delicate to handle much more.* "'Truly my soul waiteth upon God: from him cometh my salvation. He only is my rock and my salvation; he is my defense; I shall not be greatly moved.

"'How long will ye imagine mischief against a man? ye shall be slain all of you: as a bowing wall shall ye be, and as a tottering fence. They only consult to cast him down from his excellency: they delight in lies: they bless with their mouth, but they curse inwardly.

"'My soul, wait thou only upon God; for my expectation is from him. He only is my rock and my salvation: he is my defense; I shall not be moved. In God is my salvation and my glory: the rock of my strength, and my refuge, is in God. Trust in him at all times; ye people, pour out your heart before him: God is a refuge for us.' Psalm 62."

Ruth whispered the last verse with him and seemed to be calming down. It took her another couple of minutes to let go of him. When she had, Joshua quickly built up a fire. The air had started to get chilly and he hoped the fire would help cheer them both.

They slept well that night, not because of their ease of mind, but because of their complete exhaustion. Joshua woke up when the rain started hitting his face. Ugh! This was going to be a miserable day. Climbing hill after hill was bad enough without the rain. He hoped and prayed that it would stop soon.

After a small, quick breakfast, they continued climbing up and down the hills. Joshua tried his best to avoid cliffs as much as possible so Ruth wouldn't be so scared. There was little she was afraid of, but a fear of heights was one of the worst fears she had.

Joshua had no idea if they had crossed into Montana or if they were still in Wyoming. He began to despair of them reaching a town alive, as the country kept getting harder to get through.

The cliffs, hills, and ravines seemed to play with them. One ravine offering an easy route, just to have the next hill force them to backtrack. Their actual progress forward was slow. They walked a lot, but much of the time they spent going out of their way to get around a cliff or ravine.

With Ruth being deathly afraid of heights, Joshua tried to avoid going down the cliffs on a rope as much as possible.

As they trudged around yet another ravine, Joshua noticed that it had started getting dark. The sun was getting too close to the horizon. Was it really that late already? Joshua's heart sank as he looked around him. There had to be a town soon or one or both of them would go crazy.

God, please let there be a town soon. Lead us on the paths to find one.

Two days later, Joshua came to another cliff and searched the edges with his eyes, looking for an easy way down. A slight movement to his right caught his eye. His eyes narrowed as he focused in on the movement. Could it be? Was he hallucinating? It looked like smoke coming from a chimney! Not just one chimney, but a few. Yes! There was a town down there!

"Ruth! There's a town!"

Ruth jumped up from where she had been sitting on the ground waiting for Joshua to decide whether to go down or around the cliff. "Really?"

"Yes!" Joshua stepped toward her and lifted her up, twirling her around in his excitement. Ruth laughed, the sound echoing off the cliff making a sound more beautiful than a church service.

Just as fast, his mood plummeted as he realized what this meant. "Ruth," he began, his eyes keeping connected with hers, his voice hesitant, "the only way to get down there tonight is to go down the cliff on the rope."

Ruth's eyes widened in fright. "Are you sure?"

Joshua could only nod.

Ruth closed her eyes, took a deep breath, and pursed her lips. Then with a forced voice she said, "I can do it. I *will* stand strong in God's promises." She took a deep but shuddering breath before whispering, "Let's do it."

Joshua slung on his shoulder holster and rifle, then threw their bag down to the bottom of the cliff. He tied one end of the rope to a strong tree and threw the rope down to make sure it would reach the bottom. It did and he pulled it back up and started to hand the leather gloves to Ruth.

Ruth backed away from him, shaking her head. "No," she said, eyes wide. "No, I can't do it by myself. I...I c-can't."

Joshua took a deep breath and stretched his back. "Okay. We'll go down together." *God, keep my arms strong! Please!*

Ruth came up and stood as close to his back as she could. He tied the end of the rope securely around himself and Ruth.

Working together, Ruth and Joshua walked to the edge of the cliff and he lay face down with Ruth on his back. Ruth put her arms tightly around his waist as he lowered himself over the edge, keeping a tight hold on the rope. Praying for strength one more time, he lowered them down the rope.

"'I waited patiently for the Lord; and he inclined unto me, and heard my cry,'" Joshua began to quote Psalm 40 as he calculated the movements of his hands on the rope with his footholds. "'He brought me up also out of an horrible pit, out of the miry clay, and set my feet upon a rock, and established my goings. And he hath put a new song in my mouth, even praise unto our God: many shall see it and fear, and shall trust in the Lord.'"

Joshua paused to concentrate on his next foothold and Ruth picked up where he left off. She had a slight tremor in her voice, but her voice grew stronger as she recited the verses.

"'Blessed is the man that maketh the Lord his trust, and respecteth not the proud, nor such as turn aside to lies. Many, O Lord my God, are the wonderful works which thou hast done, and thy thoughts which are to us-ward: they cannot be reckoned up in order unto thee: if I would declare and speak of them, they are more than can be numbered.'"

Ruth's voice faltered and Joshua continued. "'I delight to do thy will, O my God: yea, thy law is within my heart. I have preached righteousness in the great congregation: lo, I have not refrained my lips, O Lord, thou knowest. I have not hid thy righteousness within my heart; I have declared thy faithfulness and thy salvation: I have not concealed thy lovingkindness and thy truth from the great congregation.'" That was when he saw the hungry eyes staring at them from a narrow ledge of rock.

Hanging off a cliff with your little sister trusting you to protect her and only a rope and your arms keeping you from plummeting down a cliff isn't exactly the time you would like to stare down a wolf. When he saw the wolf on a narrow ledge of the cliff, Joshua felt a frisson of fear chase up and down his spine. In an instant, he realized that Ruth would be the only one with a shot at saving them.

"Ruth," Joshua commanded, "I need you to get the rifle out and shoot that wolf who wants us for supper. I can't do it without letting go of this rope."

Joshua felt Ruth stir, stiffen, and start getting the rifle ready as she continued quoting the Psalm.

"'Withhold not thou thy tender mercies from me, O Lord: let thy lovingkindness and thy truth continually preserve me.'"

He heard the gun cock as her voice grew stronger. "'For innumerable evils have compassed me about... Be pleased, O Lord, to deliver me: O Lord, make haste to help me!'"

Joshua held them steadily level with the wolf as it continued to stare at them. Ruth's legs tightened their grip on him as she let go of his waist and held the rifle up to her shoulder.

"Cock, aim, breathe in and let it out slowly... Pull the trigger," she repeated under her breath. He heard the wolf yip before he heard the report of the rifle.

"'...I am poor and needy; yet the Lord thinketh upon me: thou art my help and my deliverer; make no tarrying, O my God.'" Ruth finished with triumph in her voice as Joshua continued working his way down the cliff.

CHAPTER TWELVE

DECEMBER 1875

SODA SPRINGS, IDAHO TERRITORY

Jed rode into Soda Springs. He'd never been to the Idaho Territory before, but he supposed there was a time for everything. A saloon caught his eye and he walked his horse up to a hitching post. He swung out of the saddle and walked to the front of his horse to tie him up.

A man came through the swinging doors just as Jed was about to walk through, and Jed had to sidestep away or risk getting run over. He pushed on a door and walked into the drink-filled room. He took a careful look around before walking up to the bar. Nobody seemed to be very threatening, so he felt almost comfortable keeping his back to most of them.

Walking up to the bar, he nodded to the bartender. "Whiskey." "A man of few words" was how one of his former partners had described him. Jed had to agree. Why say more than was necessary?

Jed placed a coin on the bar before picking up the glass of whiskey.

"You know of anybody looking to hire a man?" Jed asked after taking a slow sip of his drink.

"What'd ya do?"

"I can do most anythin'. Wranglin', cattle runnin', tendin' cattle, gunslingin', horse breakin'. I figger I've done most of it before."

The bartender bobbed his head up and down in a slow movement fitting to a man deep in thought. "Grayson. Logan Grayson needs a new ranch hand. He just had one that kilt himself. Well, not literally, but he was stupid and ended up gettin' killed."

Jed lifted the glass to his mouth and took another slow swallow. "Where can I find this Grayson?"

"Hang a left outta here, follow the road till you come to a turnoff by a stand of trees. Turn there. It's hard to miss. You'll hang a right there. Follow that till you get to the Circle LG Ranch."

Jed nodded and finished off his whiskey. "Thanks." He set the empty glass on the bar and walked out of the saloon, mounted his horse, and headed out of town.

Jed spent just less than a month on the Circle LG Ranch. Grayson needed a hand and Jed needed a job. It was a good fit, especially when his new boss found out that he was handy with a gun.

It seemed that Jed's new boss was having a bit of trouble with a couple squatters. When Logan found out that Jed was good with a gun, he asked what Jed could do about them.

"Do I get more pay if I run 'em off?" Jed asked.

Logan stared hard at Jed. "If you get rid of the squatters, you will get a bonus in your pay." His eyes held a hidden meaning that only Jed could see.

Jed nodded knowingly. "I can do it, but I gotta get a few things from town."

Logan assented and Jed rode for town minutes later. When he came back, he packed bread and jerky in his saddlebags then packed them and a bedroll on a packhorse.

"You take to a job real fast, Stuart." Logan stood leaning on a fence rail.

Jed cringed inside. He hated how Logan used his men's last names instead of their first. If he'd known about it, he would've told his new boss a different last name. "I figger the sooner I get rid of the squatters, the sooner I can leave."

"You're leaving?"

"You only hired me for a month. I just figgered I'd be leavin'."

Logan nodded. "If I were to hire you longer, would you stay?"

Jed shook his head. "Nope. I got things I need to take care of first. I only took this job 'cuz I needed the money to finish what I was doin'." He tightened the rope on the gray packhorse and turned to rub his saddle horse down.

Logan watched in silence. "Get this job of the squatters done, and I'll let you be on your way to attend to your unfinished business."

Jed shot a quick glance at his boss. "Yes, Sir." He set the brush aside and swung into the saddle. After touching the brim of his hat, he nudged his horse into a trot, holding on to the packhorse's lead rope.

Jed let his horse take its time as he made a methodical search of the Grayson land. The sun was beginning to set when he spotted a hill that would overlook the property. He hoped he would be able to see at least one of the squatter's camps. As he searched his memory for a general lay of the land, he thought the area on the other side of the hill would be a perfect spot for a squatter's camp. Three hours after leaving the ranch house, Jed reached the top of the hill giving him a view of one of the squatter's camps. His quick scan of the camp showed four men, four horses, and two pack mules. They had started building a small cabin, but were still camping out by their large fire.

Four against one. Pretty good odds, though I still have the advantage. I know I'm coming and they don't.

He picketed his horses just on the other side of the hill and sat at the top of the hill to observe. If there was one thing he had learned in his life, it was to wait for his opportunities.

Jed observed the camp until night began to fall. He took his pistol and rifle and worked his way down the hill, staying in the shadows. Two of the men moved away from the camp. Jed assumed they meant to get water and wood for the night, just as he had hoped would happen. He followed them as they headed for the creek. The two men ambled along a couple dozen yards chatting and laughing together.

They were about halfway to the creek when one of the men turned his head away from Jed and toward his partner. They stopped walking and had an animated discussion that lasted forty seconds by Jed's count. Jed was too far away to hear what they were saying, but from their gestures, he guessed that they were about to split up, one to get the water and the other some wood. When one of the men started moving a different direction, Jed made a quick decision.

"Stay right where you are," Jed hissed.

Both men spun around, drawing their guns as they turned. Jed was too quick for them and the two gunshots were heard as one. Both men dropped to the ground. Jed moved in the direction of the camp, keeping off the path. Angry that his plan hadn't gone the way he wanted, he fumed in his subconscious while trying to stay alert. He had always hated the feeling that came after killing a man, but they had drawn on him first and out here in the West that was as good as signing a death wish if you were a good hand with a gun. As he walked back toward the camp, he thought back to his plan. Kill when necessary, otherwise just run 'em off.

He heard men running toward him and stepped into the middle of the path, gun drawn. The two remaining squatters stopped in their tracks.

"What do you want?" the taller, grizzled man sneered.

"You're squattin' on my boss's land. He don't take too kindly to that."

The shorter man coughed in derision. "So he sent you to take care of us? All four of us?"

Jed stared the man in the eyes, daring him to look away. He did. "Yes, all four of you. Two are already dead."

"Impossible!" the tall man scoffed. "There was only one gunshot."

"There were two." Jed looked at the taller man. *I believe he is the leader of the group.* "You have two options. One, draw your guns and try to outgun me; or two, take your horses and leave immediately. If you choose the second one and I, or some other

130

cowpoke, ever sees your sorry hides again, we will shoot first and ask questions later."

"Can we bury our friends first, then leave?"

Jed nodded. "Be outta here in two hours or I will kill you both."

The two men turned on their heels and headed back to their camp. Jed hurried back to his observation point and followed their movements. They were smart men and he commended them. They were gone long before their two hours had been spent.

Jed walked back to his horses, rolled out his bedroll, and lay down for some much needed sleep. He could only hope the next two camps of squatters would be this easy. *If Logan'd known it would be this easy, he wouldn't've sent me out here. He could've done it himself.* Jed shook his head. He knew he had gotten lucky. The other camps wouldn't be so easy. He just hoped he didn't get killed in the process. After all, he still had two kids to find.

A week later, Jed rode back into the ranch yard. His beard and hair were more scraggly than before and he was covered in dust from head to foot.

Logan stood in the paddock saddling his horse when Jed rode into the ranch yard. "Jed! Done already?"

"Yep. No more squatters on yer land."

Logan reached for the reins. "I'll take care of the horses. You go get cleaned up and rested."

Jed shook his head. "I'll finish what I started."

Logan stepped back to watch as Jed hiked his stiff right leg over the saddle. He grimaced when his legs hit the ground. Taking a deep breath, he forced his legs and arms to move. Jed made quick work of unsaddling and brushing down the horses. As he led his horses into the barn, he realized with a start that Logan had disappeared. *Good,* Jed thought. *At least I don't have him looking over my shoulder while I work the kinks out of my sore body.*

When his horses were taken care of, Jed washed up in the creek before heading to the bunkhouse.

After supper, Logan told Jed to join him in his office.

"You did a good job, Stuart. I would be happy to hire you again if you are ever in need of a job and in the area. Meanwhile, I stick to my promise. Here is your one month's wages and the bonus. You can leave when you are ready."

"Thank you, Grayson." Jed turned to leave.

"How many squatters were there?"

"Four in the first camp, five in the second one, and two in the third."

Logan looked puzzled for a couple of seconds, but quickly recovered.

"I told 'em you would kill 'em on sight if they ever showed their faces around here."

Logan nodded. "I'll keep an eye out, but will most likely just have to take their words for it since I haven't seen 'em." He smiled.

Jed blinked his eyes. "Right. I hadn't thought of that." He shrugged. "I doubt you'll see any of 'em anyway. If you've any more problems with squatters, just send a couple of your men out to search 'em out an warn 'em off. You don't usually need a gunfighter for that."

"Thank you for taking care of things for me."

Jed simply nodded and left the den, his mind already on where he would go next. He decided to go northwest again and see what he could find out. There had to be a way to find the kids without raising suspicions and Jed was determined to find it.

CHAPTER THIRTEEN

EARLY NOVEMBER 1875
MONTANA TERRITORY

Joshua got them to the bottom of the cliff safe and sound and immediately went to check that the wolf was dead. When that was taken care of, he picked up their pack and they hurried toward the town. The sun was beginning to set behind the hills when they arrived. They stopped at the head of the street to get their bearings and moved to the side when they saw a man heading out of town on horseback. Joshua was about to let him pass by them when the sun glinted off the star on his chest.

"Sheriff?" Joshua called.

The sheriff looked back at him. "Can it wait a half hour? Someone told of a gunshot heard outside of town."

"When was that?"

"Ten or fifteen minutes ago."

Joshua nodded. "You don't need to investigate, Sir. My sister shot a timber wolf that was after us."

The sheriff stared at Joshua and Ruth, disbelief written all over his face.

Joshua sighed. "It's a long story, Sir. We also have to report a stagecoach robbery."

The sheriff dismounted and stood directly in front of Joshua, staring him in the eyes. "When was the robbery?"

"Just over a week ago, Sir." Joshua couldn't believe how talking to the sheriff seemed to release all the exhaustion that had built up over the last week. It was as if his body decided to shut down now that he was safe.

The sheriff looked at the siblings. His eyes took in their very bedraggled appearance. "The robbery was over a week ago? Do you have any idea where?"

"Somewhere between Casper, Wyoming, and Bozeman, Montana, Sir. We left Cheyenne early morning and traveled until midafternoon. We were headed for the station at Preston."

"How long's it been since you two had a good meal and comfortable place to sleep?"

"A long time, Sheriff," Ruth sighed.

"I'll take you over to McCourdy's boarding house and you can have something to eat and get some rest. We can talk about the robbery in the morning."

"Thank you, Sir," Joshua said.

Mrs. McCourdy, a sweet older lady, immediately took them under her wing.

"The sheriff told me all about what happened to you two," she started, her hands making odd movements every few seconds. "It's a shame what some of those young men think to take on with their lives. If they would just find something honorable to do, there would be a lot less heartache. That's what I think."

Joshua and Ruth exchanged an amused glance behind Mrs. McCourdy's back as she ushered them down the hall, one on either side of her.

"Okay, I have these two rooms for you. You two will be right next to each other. I have water heating for baths. When you are ready, you can come downstairs. Unfortunately, I can't give you each a bath in your room."

Joshua held his hand up. "Don't worry about that, Ma'am. We wouldn't know what to do if we could have a bath in our own room." He grinned.

Mrs. McCourdy's smile broadened and she tittered. "Well then, I shan't worry about it. I do have two tubs and screens enough for both of you, so if you are ready at the same time, you can both bathe at the same time." She paused for a couple of seconds. "Oh yes, and I will find you something clean to wear. It might be a little big on you, but it will be better than what you have right now."

"Thank you—" Ruth began.

"And," Mrs. McCourdy interrupted, "I will have a hot meal for you by the time you are clean." By this time, she had both doors open. "Very good. I will see you downstairs in a jiffy."

Joshua and Ruth suppressed their laugh of amusement as she disappeared back down the hall.

"She's so sweet," Ruth said. "I wish she were my grandmother."

Joshua nodded. "She is a character, that's for sure."

Joshua and Ruth got themselves comfortable in their rooms and then headed down to the kitchen and their baths. They soaked in their tubs as long as they dared before putting the clean clothes on and eating a home-cooked meal.

Full of good food and clean for the first time in weeks, and exhausted, Joshua and Ruth collapsed on their beds and were instantly asleep.

The next morning, Joshua awoke to the smell of coffee and bacon. He sniffed the tempting air as he dressed in the clean clothes by his bed. The pants were a little short and the shirt too wide in the shoulders, but otherwise they fit pretty well. "What luxury!" he told himself as he breathed in deeply. "I will never take coffee and bacon for granted again."

As he left his room, he saw Ruth coming out in a dress that actually seemed to fit her pretty well.

"You look good," she said with a smile.

"So do you," Joshua replied.

She sniffed in his direction. "You smell decent, too."

Joshua batted at her playfully. "It's amazing what a bath can do," he retorted.

Ruth laughed. "Let's go eat. I'm starved."

"I'm not starved, I'm famished. Race you."

"You can run like a boy if you want, but I am going to walk like a lady," Ruth said with a superior air, her nose in the air.

Joshua stopped midstride and stood to his full height. "Why, whatevah was I thinking?" he said in an exaggerated accent. "I must be more gentlemanly." He bowed to his sister. "Aftah you, deah sistah." He held out his arm.

"Why thank you, brother dear," she said as she laid her arm on his as though she was a lady in a ballroom. They walked into the dining room together.

After a delicious breakfast of eggs, bacon, fried potatoes, and hotcakes, Ruth and Joshua headed over to the sheriff's office.

The sheriff sat at his desk, writing, when they entered. He looked up and stood. "I trust you slept well last night."

"Yes, thank you very much, Sir."

139

The sheriff nodded his acknowledgment before holding his hand out to Joshua. "Sheriff Carlton."

Joshua shook his hand. "Joshua Brookings. My sister, Ruth."

The sheriff gestured toward the straight back chairs across from his desk. "Please have a seat." Joshua and Ruth each sat on a chair. "Let's get right down to business. What can you tell me about the robbery?"

Joshua sat back, silently contemplating how to begin. Should he make it dramatic or just matter-of-fact? He decided on a slight compromise between the two. "The day began as usual: a quick meal at the stage stop and then back into the stage for another bumpy ride. We went on as usual until midafternoon. Then we stopped. There was a big tree in the road, blocking the way. I started to get out of the coach when I heard other voices.

"They wanted the strongbox. I don't think it was going to be a murderous robbery, but the shotgun guard and driver refused to let them have the strongbox. One of the men came to the passenger door to steal our valuables, but we didn't have any. I'm not really sure what he was planning on doing with us, because he got distracted by something happening up front. Ruth and I went around the back of the stage and to the other side.

"I decided we would try to make a run for it. We went out the door and hid in the woods. Ruth got her journal and pencil out to write down the descriptions of the outlaws I gave her. As I finished giving her the descriptions, I noticed one of the men cock his gun. There was shooting and one of the robbers was killed by the driver after the guard was shot. I shot one of the outlaws, wounding him. Both the driver and the guard were killed before I could get a clean shot at the only other outlaw still uninjured.

"We left the area and started running, knowing they would be after us. We lost the man tracking us after about two or three days. We were about ready to despair of ever finding a town when we saw this one from on top of the cliff. The stage is gone; who knows what they did with it."

"What happened to the bodies?" Sheriff Carlton asked.

"We didn't stay long enough to find out what they did."

Sheriff Carlton nodded. "Do you have the descriptions with you?"

Ruth opened her reticule and pulled out a piece of paper. She stood up and walked to his desk. "Here they are. I also have a letter for the wife of the driver. Can you get it to her?"

Sheriff Carlton took the letter and nodded. "Where were you two headed?"

"Cartersville, Montana."

"The next stage leaves here tomorrow at noon. I telegraphed the owners and they said you two should be on it and you can have the driver drop you off right at your house."

Ruth's eyes filled with tears. "Thank you," she whispered.

"Where is the telegraph office?" Joshua asked.

"Take a right out of here and go two doors down the street." Sheriff Carlton paused. "If I need anything more, I will try to think of it before tomorrow at noon." He smiled. "I'll let you go now. Do you need anything before you head to Cartersville?"

Joshua thought. "Just some clothes, but these'll do until we get to Pa and Ma."

Sheriff Carlton nodded and Joshua led his sister to the telegraph office. They sent two short telegrams. One to Matthew saying that they had run into a little trouble, but would be joining up with their parents soon. The other telegram went to their parents telling them when they would arrive.

The stagecoach ride was uneventful and when they finally saw the land their parents had purchased with their pa and ma standing at the edge of the road waiting for them, Ruth got teary-eyed and Joshua had a hard time breathing. The stagecoach wheels were still turning when Joshua opened the door, jumped off the stage without waiting for the block, swung his sister out, and ran to hug his parents. All four of them wept unashamedly with joy at the sight of each other.

Pa finally noticed the embarrassed driver and guard next to the bag. "Thank you for dropping them off."

The driver nodded. "Not a problem." He and the guard climbed back onto the stage and drove away.

Joshua took a quick look around, noticing that somehow, even though he had never set eyes on this property before, it felt like home. The brown grass, the rolling hills, the trees all seemed familiar. He turned his excited gaze to his parents. Drinking in the sight of his mother in her tasteful, though faded, calico dress and his father in his denim pants and cotton shirt, he closed his eyes and breathed a quick prayer of thanks before speaking.

"Let's see the place you bought!" Joshua said, excitement sparkling in his eyes. "Then we have a long tale to tell you."

Ruth laughed. "A very long tale. One I never, ever want to repeat in real life again!"

Joshua grinned at her. "But we lived, didn't we?"

"By God's grace, we did."

CHAPTER FOURTEEN

Dear Diary,

We finally made it home. Ma and Pa were as glad to see us as we were to see them. It was a wonderful, precious reunion. We told them everything about our trip. As we told them the story, we found out that they had been praying for us continually. God had even woken them up during the night a couple of times.

After telling them our story, we spent an hour praising God for His care. Then Joshua finally got his wish: to see the ranch! When Pa bought the land, it came with a small cabin with a kitchen/living area, two small bedrooms downstairs, and a loft. Joshua claimed the loft, which was just fine with me.

We took a short tour of the outside, but it started getting dark so we couldn't see very much. The barn looked really nice and the horses and cow seemed to like it.

Tomorrow we plan on riding the horses all over the land. Pa said we can see the mountains in the distance from the top of one of the hills. His dream is to build a house up there with a big window facing the mountains. Ma got really dreamy-eyed when he said that. I hope he can do it.

Well, I should get some sleep so I can be well rested for tomorrow's ride.

Ruth

Dear Diary,

Yesterday was great! The ride was so relaxing and the farm is so beautiful. There's a lot of work that needs to be done, but the potential is amazing! We started out toward where Pa envisions the pastures being. I could almost see the fence lines and all the horses and cattle grazing on the lush green grass.

There is a stream that wanders through the pasture area. It is so clear. Pa thinks it comes straight from the mountains. We have a lot of hills. Some steep, some with gentle slopes, some barely able to be called hills.

"This hill," Pa said after a half hour, "is the hill that our house will be going on." He jumped off his horse and started pacing the dimensions. "It will be two stories tall with lots of windows looking out over...there." He swept his arm to the northwest.

We all gasped in amazement at the beauty of the snow-covered blue mountains. Oh, Father, thank You so much for blessing us with this beautiful land! It was worth everything we went through to be able to see this.

I have been committed to be content in all circumstances, whether easy or hard. This place will make it easy!

We certainly have a lot of hard work ahead of us, but we are together and, working together, we will get it done. Thank You, God, for Your wonderful grace to us poor, miserable sinners.

Ruth

Dear Diary,

It has been a few days since I last wrote. I have been busy! We started clearing the land of brush as well as planting some flower bulbs, and getting Joshua and me settled in our new rooms. Pa is going to start building the fences tomorrow. Soon we will be able to get our first cattle!

Ma and I have been able to do some talking. It is so nice to be back with her again. We were separated for a whole year. I cannot imagine being separated from her for even longer. I would never be able to survive.

Tomorrow, Mom and I are going to visit our nearest neighbors. They live about a mile away. It will be nice to meet some more people. Mom said they have a girl my age. I hope I like her. It would be nice to have a friend that lives within such easy walking distance.

Ruth

Ruth laughed when she saw the face her mother, Harriet Brookings, made as she started to tell her about the first time she met their neighbors.

"I was so intimidated," Harriet said, "when I walked up to the house in my dirty calico and saw Mrs. Wilson's dress." She turned her face toward Ruth. "It was a green satin and had obviously been made to order from the East in one of the latest fashions. It was full of lace and embroidery like you have never seen. I felt like a lowly servant and I was wearing one of my best dresses!" Harriet laughed. "But, behind the satin and lace, Mrs. Wilson has a heart of gold. She never mentioned my dress once and she certainly did not look down on me."

Ruth sighed. "I hope her daughter is as nice."

Harriet drew her lips together. "Me, too. I never saw her since she wasn't feeling quite herself when I visited. But, from Mrs. Wilson's description, you two should be able to find something in common."

The mother and daughter stopped talking as they walked up the path to the door. Mrs. Wilson answered and ushered them in. "I am so glad you brought your daughter today, Harriet," she gushed. "Annabelle has been talking of little else since I told her that Ruth would be coming for a visit soon."

"Ruth was excited to hear that there was a girl her age within walking distance, weren't you, Ruth?"

Ruth tore her eyes away from Mrs. Wilson's brilliant royal blue dress. "Yes, Mama, I was." She allowed a slight smile to peek out.

"Here we are," Mrs. Wilson announced. "Annabelle, this is Ruth and Harriet Brookings. Ruth and Harriet, my daughter, Annabelle."

Ruth had thought Mrs. Wilson's dress was extravagant, but when she saw Annabelle's, it was all she could do not to let her jaw drop to the floor. Then she caught Annabelle's eyes as they scanned her dress. Annabelle gave a quiet sigh and seemed to dismiss her as unworthy of her attention.

Ruth's chest tightened. Did she really look that bad? Was she really that far beneath Annabelle Wilson?

Ruth forced a smile to her lips and walked closer to Annabelle. She held out a hand. "Hello, Annabelle. How are you today?"

Annabelle looked at Ruth's hand before taking it in hers with the barest of touches. "Not too bad, though this cold is getting to me. I fear I'll take to my bed with a head cold any day now."

"Do you suffer from head colds often? Mama has a surefire cure for them."

Annabelle rolled her eyes. "That won't be necessary. I wouldn't want to bother her with it."

"Oh, it's no bother," Ruth said. "She loves to help people, especially if it will help them to get over a recurring illness."

Annabelle shook her head. "No, I don't need it. I am sick of medicines."

Ruth and Annabelle sat in silence while Ruth waited for Annabelle to continue the conversation. When she didn't, Ruth knew that her first impression had been correct. Annabelle wanted nothing to do with her.

"What is your favorite way to pass the time?" Ruth asked.

"Looking at the latest Godey's Lady's Book and sometimes reading."

"I love reading! What books do you like to read? Who is your favorite author?"

"I like anything with romance in it. I don't have a favorite author."

Ruth sighed as silently as possible. It was almost impossible to keep up a conversation when the other half of the conversing pair refused to ask questions and then when they answered a question, they kept the answer as brief as possible.

Ruth decided to give up and turned to listen to the conversation the mothers were having together. As she turned her head, her eye caught the bookshelf standing in the corner. She breathed in a gasp of delight and walked over to it before she even realized she had stood up.

She skimmed the titles and touched the bindings with the reverence of a true book connoisseur.

She was startled out of her reverie by Mrs. Wilson's voice.

"Some of those books are over a hundred years old. My husband likes to collect books no matter what they are about." She let out a short laugh. "I don't know if anybody has read all the books on that shelf."

"If Ruth had a shelf like that, she would have read all the books within the year. At least once."

"Mama!" Ruth turned with a blush. "I don't read that much."

Harriet laughed. "Not quite that much, but you do read a lot."

Ruth turned back to the shelf to hide her hot cheeks while Harriet and Mrs. Wilson chatted about being rancher's wives. When she found a book she hadn't read in a long time, she took it off the shelf and brought it back to the couch she had been sitting on.

"What book did you find?" Annabelle asked. "I thought Father only had old, dry books up there."

Ruth smiled. "No, some of them sound very interesting. This is a very old version of *Pilgrim's Progress* by John Bunyan. I haven't read it in over a year and thought I could possibly skim through some of my favorite parts. Have you ever read *Pilgrim's Progress*?"

Annabelle raised an eyebrow. "Me? No, I most certainly have not. Isn't it some sort of religious book?"

"Yes, it is an allegory of the Christian life. It is much more interesting than the title might suggest."

Annabelle sniffed. "You won't catch me ever reading any religious book."

Ruth stared at Annabelle, her eyes wide and mouth trying to drop open. "Why not?"

"Religion is fine for some people, but there is no way I will ever need a crutch to get through life. I have my parents, plenty of money, and I live a good life. I do my best to be good. God will have to just be fine with that."

Ruth was speechless as Annabelle spoke. She had heard those sentiments, or thoughts similar to them, before. But those had always been from someone older. Someone at least thirty years old. Not from a sixteen year old.

Just as she was about to try to answer Annabelle's declaration, Harriet spoke, "Ruth dear, we should head back home. It is starting to cloud over and we don't want to get caught out in a storm."

Ruth nodded and stepped over to the shelf to put the book back. Once the book was in place, she turned to Annabelle. "It was nice meeting you, Annabelle. I hope you can come visit us soon. I would enjoy getting to know you better."

Annabelle took a quick glance at her mother and spoke in an undertone. "I doubt that. We have nothing in common and are as alike as an apple and a carrot. But, if Mother goes visiting, I'll most likely join her."

Harriet and Mrs. Wilson had already said goodbye and Mrs. Wilson ushered them to the door.

Ruth and Harriet walked home in silence. Ruth wondered why her ma didn't talk to her, but she guessed that Harriet had read her mood and knew that she needed some time to think before talking about her afternoon. When she arrived home, she went straight to her room and picked up her diary to write.

Dear Diary,

Well, having a friend so close may simply be a dream. Annabelle is not very friendly. When we got to the house, she barely said hello and completely ignored all my attempts at conversation. I guess she simply wanted to listen in on what our mothers were talking about.

I don't want to sound like I'm complaining, but what are diaries for if I don't say exactly what I am feeling? She made me feel like I was inferior. She wore a very pretty dress that would have been the envy of all the girls back East. She acted snooty and uppity. She acted as if I were dirt poor and she owned millions.

Just because I don't have a fancy dress does not mean I am poor! I wouldn't be caught dead wearing a dress like that out here, unless it was to a dance or some formal event. My calico dress is much more practical.

I am disappointed, but I will pray for Annabelle and hopefully we can become friends, eventually.

Ruth

CHAPTER FIFTEEN

1876

WYOMING, MONTANA, AND IDAHO TERRITORIES

Jed rode northwest, stopping in every town he came across. In town, he would try to ask questions about the kids. He couldn't believe how hard it was to ask questions without people getting suspicious. Though he knew he looked like a gunman and that gunmen weren't always trusted, he'd thought getting answers would've been a little easier.

When answers were hard to get, he turned to the people who knew everything that went on in town and would not say a word about who asked or why. The only problem being that he needed a lot of money to pay the saloon girls to answer his questions. This meant he had to work hard to earn a few measly dollars here and there to find out any information.

A month went by and he had still found nothing about the kids. If only he had their names! His money had started to run low and he was getting desperate. His anger boiled just below the surface the more time passed. He had tried contacting Garrett and Tom through secret means, but had received no response. That either meant they were dead or long gone. Which also meant he was completely alone in the world.

Not that he minded being alone, but a friend, even a dubious friend like Tom or Garrett, had been somehow comforting. As far as Jed knew, no one in the world cared whether he lived or died.

Your sister cares, a demon in him said. Jed's blood froze at the thought. No, he couldn't think of Anna. Anna might care about him, but that meant nothing. She meant nothing to him. He shook his head violently.

The bartender looked over at him. "You okay, Mister?"

Jed nodded and sipped his whiskey. He had to get a hold of himself, but not right now. Maybe tomorrow. He spent the afternoon and night drinking one thing after another. By the time he left the saloon, he was drunk and mad. The drinks hadn't blocked the kids from his thoughts. If anything, it made the thoughts worse. The face of the girl from the stage seemed to be stuck in front of him. He was angry at the world and was ready to take his anger out on the first person or thing he met.

As he walked back to his camp outside Cheyenne, he saw a lithe, womanly figure slipping along the street. His eyes narrowed and he hurried toward her. As he got closer, he took in her clothing. She seemed too well clothed to be a normal lady of the night, but right now, he didn't care.

He grabbed her arm and quickly put a hand to her mouth, stifling the girl's scream. "Don't make a sound." He dragged her out of town to his camp. Once there, he sat her down against a tree and tied her up before building a fire.

"What're you going to do with me?" she spat once the fire was built and they could see each other.

Jed raised an eyebrow. This girl was a little spitfire. "What're you doin' out of your house, Little Lady? You don't quite seem the prostitute type."

The girl lifted her chin, but said nothing.

"Do you have a name, Girl?"

Jed could almost feel the flames coming from her eyes.

"Why does it matter?" she asked.

Jed shrugged. "It just does. Tell me or things'll be worse for you."

"Elizabeth Harris." The fear he knew she had to be feeling started showing in her voice and he felt his face twisting into an evil smile.

"Well, Miss Elizabeth Harris. Are you ready for an education you never would have dreamed of?"

"No, I'm not," she replied. Her voice trembled and Jed felt a tiny stab of regret, but quickly squelched it and walked over to the tree to untie Elizabeth.

When Jed woke up the next morning, he felt like he was sitting in a mine full of men pounding away with their picks and dynamite. It felt like the heavy rocks were inside his head getting moved with as much banging together as possible from his head to his heart, making his load of guilt feel even heavier. He had known what he was doing was wrong. *Why did I take my anger out on that girl?*

Even though he had been drunk half out of his mind, he should have still had enough sense to know he was wrong before he ever started. But for some reason, he'd been unable to stop himself. He cursed himself, he cursed the kids, and he cursed the law that would surely be after him. He had to disappear. Lie low for a while. Get out of the area.

Jed looked around him through his unfocused eyes. *Even drunk, I knew I was wrong. So much so that I somehow got the girl back to town and then got outta town without killing myself.*

Jed rose from his hard bed with slow, deliberate movements. His head had been pounding since he woke up and the bright sun didn't help any. But he had to keep moving. He had to get out of there before the law came after him.

Jed blinked his eyes, trying to make sense of what his eyes were telling him. Scrub brush, sand, a road. The town wasn't far away. And of course he would have been stupid enough to pick a town that the U.S. Marshal stationed. Jed swung his leg over the saddle, being careful not to jar his head, then urged Copper forward.

It's those kids that're doin' this to me, he thought as he trotted away from Cheyenne, one of the fastest growing cattle towns of the West. *They caused me to do this. I was doin' fine until I met up with 'em and they kilt off my partners. Now I've no one in the whole world to stop me. I will do as I please, when I please, and where I please.* He grimaced when his horse stumbled, jostling him. If only he didn't hurt so much, this trip wouldn't be half-bad.

His headache had started to ease a little, but his head still pounded unbearably. Although he was half-Irish, and the Irish were known for their drinking, Jed had done his best to avoid the stuff. His father had always drunk too much and Jed did most anything to be as unlike his da as possible.

Then he had met those kids. He scowled to himself. He'd had too many last night and now he suffered the consequences. "It's all those kids' fault!" he yelled. "If only I could get my hands on them!" His voice lowered into a threatening growl. "I'd teach 'em then. I'd teach 'em to cross Jed Stuart."

From Cheyenne, Jed wandered toward Montana. Fueled by his anger, hatred, and guilt, he kept to the shadiest parts of town. In an almost constant state of drunkenness, trying to forget, but never fully being able to. He was too Irish! He cursed his mother's Irish blood for giving him an Irish stomach that held beer too well. Because of it, he could not get as drunk as he wanted.

Jed took odd jobs along the way to nowhere. Desperate ranchers hired him to watch their cattle. Unscrupulous men hired him to kill somebody or to be a bodyguard to keep them safe. His name became a byword in gunslinger fame. At least for a few months. Maybe a year. Until someone better than him would come along and steal the fame.

Jed always felt better after these last jobs were completed. Helping people get rid of problems somehow helped ease the anger for a few days. Then the questions would come back. No amount of drinking could block the questions.

He had just helped to stop a range war. The law hadn't been too happy about his part in it, but he didn't care what they thought. Jed walked his horse into the nearby town and the questions flooded his mind again. Why did the kids have to get away? Why did his mother die? Why couldn't his da have loved him? Why had he started drinking? Why hadn't he just let Tom kill him when they'd first met? Why had he done anything? Why bother living anymore?

Something caught his attention on his right. The horse missed a step at the subtle movement from Jed. Jed stared at the building. A church? There was actually something so...civilized out here in this two-bit town? He scoffed at the idea and started mumbling under his breath, "That must be a really dumb man. Either that or a really brave man to be so crazy as to start a church way out here."

As Jed urged his horse past the church, another set of questions started coming. Why was God so distant? Why had God forsaken him?

Maybe you should ask the minister, a voice in him said. Jed shook his head in frustration. Never! Never, ever would he turn religious! Religion was a waste of time. Why bother with it?

Two nights later, Jed waited for the moon to set and darkness to settle on the land. He and his horse stood in a clump of trees on a hill. The hill overlooked a sprawling cattle ranch. The moon's last beams showed just above a distant hill and Jed swung into his saddle. With a whisper, he got Copper moving down the hill to the farthest pasture.

His shrewd eyes found a few stray head of cattle. He took another quick glance around. No one in sight. Copper cut some of the cattle from the edge of the herd and guided them away from their former home and to a new pasture.

With Copper's help, Jed herded the seven head of cattle onto the land he would be temporarily calling his own. As he neared the corral he had built, he noticed two men looking around his place.

"Howdy!" he greeted them with false welcome. "What'cha doin' on my land?"

"Just seein' what's goin' on here," the taller of the two said. "No one was at the house, so we thought we'd see what kinda place this was. Is there a problem with that?"

Jed kept his hand near his pistol and held the reins loosely in his left hand. He looked the two men over in the darkness. "Nope," Jed said. "I s'pose there isn't." Deciding the two men didn't mean immediate harm to him, he moved the cattle into the corral.

Once they were secure, he dismounted, rubbed down his horse, took the saddle off, and let the horse into his own pasture.

"Where you two headed?" Jed asked.

"Nowhere's in particular," the shorter man said.

"You need a place to stay the night?" Jed asked before he thought. "It ain't much, but I got a roof and some blankets. I might even be able to scrounge up some grub in the mornin'." Jed was thankful for the darkness as he scowled to himself. *Why did I say that? And why in the world am I bein' so nice to these two strangers? For all I know, they were sent here by the Marshal in Cheyenne come to get me and drag me off to jail!*

"We'd be mighty obliged," the tall man answered.

The two men led their horses to the pasture and Jed grabbed some wood as they all headed into the shack. He dropped the wood in the wood box and struck a match to light the lamp on the crude table. He searched around for some food and found a couple cans of beans and some jerky. One of the men built a fire and soon had it crackling. They sat down to eat the jerky and cold beans while the coffee brewed.

Jed took a good look at the two men in front of him. Now that they were in the light, they seemed familiar. "Do I know you two?"

The taller man chuckled. "What're the odds? We're the squatters you ran off Grayson's land a few months back."

Jed blinked his eyes in disbelief, then shook his head. "The name's Jed."

"Walter," the tall man offered. "And my brother, Charles."

They continued to eat in silence for a few minutes.

"Those cattle you were bringin' into the corral. Where'd you get them?" Charles asked.

Jed narrowed his eyes as he looked up at him. "Why?"

"We figgered they were probably rustled. Where else do you get cattle in the middle of the night?" Walter asked. "Anyway, we was just wonderin'. If they were, we might like to join you. If you'll have us. Rustlin' cattle is more profitable with more than one person."

Jed leaned back in his chair, lifting it up off the front legs, and studied the brothers. "So you two want to join me in my lawless deeds?" Jed asked.

"Like we ain't done plenty of lawless things in our lives before?" Walter chuckled again.

Charles grunted. "If you'll have us, we wouldn't mind settlin' down to steady work for a bit."

Jed set his chair back on all fours and stared at the fire in thought. *Was it a setup? Nah. Lawmen wouldn't be so obvious. And they do look to be brothers. And they was squattin' on Grayson's land before.* He took a quick glance at them. *'Course, that could give 'em reason to hate me since I killed two of their partners.*

Jed eyed the two men. "Why should I trust you? Last time we met, I had just killed two of your buddies."

Charles raised an eyebrow. "Right. I'd forgotten about that." He cleared his throat. "Those two were

166

guys we'd just met up with and we just wanted to make sure they had a decent burial."

Walter nodded. "That's right. We were just glad you let us go."

Jed glanced between the brothers before returning his gaze to the fire. "All right, you two can join me. I'd be glad for the help. But one wrong move on either of your parts and I shoot first and ask questions later."

Charles and Walter each offered a hand to Jed and they shook on their deal.

And so a partnership of crime began.

CHAPTER SIXTEEN

1876

DOUBLE B RANCH, CARTERSVILLE,
MONTANA TERRITORY

The next few months flew by. Ruth and Joshua
worked beside their parents getting things ready to
put fences in, and getting the house in order.
Christmas came and went with a small celebration
and reminiscences about past Christmases. The New
Year rang in without acknowledgment from the
Brookings family.

As the weather began to warm up, Daniel
Brookings went into town to buy the milled wood
for the buildings. The man asked him what he
planned on building.

"We've got a barn or two and a bunkhouse to
build," Daniel said.

"You want some help with it?"

"You know somebody who needs some work?"
Daniel asked, curiosity blooming in his face.

"Nope," the man said. "But, I know the folks 'round here love a barn raisin'. It's 'bout the only time the whole community gets together to work on a project and have a bit of a dance."

Daniel Brookings grinned. "Sounds good to me. Can you spread the word?"

"Yep. Got a specific day you'd like to do it?"

"Do you think this Friday would work?"

The man worked the chewing tobacco in his mouth for a minute. "I don't see why not. I'll tell folks to be out there. Just so's ya know, the women'll be bringin' food. Your wife don't have to feed all of us."

Daniel waved a hand to him. "Thank you for your help."

"No problem. That's what neighbors are for, ain't it?"

Daniel laughed with him, climbed into the loaded wagon, and headed back to the ranch.

Early Friday morning, Ruth and her mother were hard at work in the kitchen. Despite Daniel's reassurance that there would be plenty of food, Harriet was still determined to make doubly sure there was enough.

Two hours after sunrise, wagon loads of men, women, and children began to arrive. Harriet got the women and food organized, and chatted with the women. Ruth scurried around being helpful and trying to stay in the background.

Daniel and Joshua got the men organized into eight work crews. Four crews would work on the barn and the other four would work on the bunkhouse. Daniel put Joshua in charge of the crews working on the bunkhouse and Daniel took charge of the barn.

By noon, the buildings were well on their way to being finished. The crews took a welcome break to eat the vittles brought in by the women. Joshua and Daniel were engaged in many different conversations with the men helping them. Harriet and Ruth kept busy making sure that no empty dishes stayed on the makeshift tables.

Four hours after lunch, the last board was nailed into the bunkhouse and the barn was only a half hour away from completion. After a quick dinner, one of the men pulled out a fiddle, another man grabbed his washboard, and a boy pulled out a harmonica. The fiddler took charge and started playing a lively song and calling out the steps for a square dance. Young people and old alike hurried into the new barn and formed their squares.

Ruth hung back on the edges of the crowd and watched the dancing. Joshua joined the dancers and enjoyed himself, dancing with whoever was available. At one point, Ruth allowed her father to talk her into joining one of the dances, but otherwise stayed away from the dance floor. She preferred to watch.

Ruth spotted Annabelle nearby and they talked for a few minutes, giving Ruth a glimmer of hope that they might just become friends.

As the sun set and darkness settled on the land, more and more people gathered their belongings and children and left for their homes.

As the last person left, Ruth heard Daniel remark, "Well, that was a productive day."

Joshua laughed. "I would say so. I can't imagine how long it would have taken if we hadn't had so much help."

Ruth smiled. "We have good neighbors and I think a lot of new friendships were formed today for us."

Harriet yawned. "Yes, but I'm beat. I think I will head in and ignore all the dishes that need washed. We can finish them in the morning."

They all traipsed into the house and collapsed into their beds.

Four months after the barn raising most of the fences were built, the bunkhouse was ready, and the barn was full of hay. Daniel and Joshua rode to the capital city, Helena, to find a few ranch hands and scout out some places to buy horses.

After arriving in the West, Daniel realized that as profitable as cattle were, horses were even more profitable if you had enough money and land to cover the startup costs. He planned to buy some good breeding stock and get a good start with them. Then he and his hands would find some of the wild herds and capture and gentle many of their horses from those herds.

He figured it would take a couple of years before he had enough horses to start selling them, but when he did, he would sell them to the Army, the ranchers, the Indians, and anyone else who needed or wanted a horse.

"I can't wait to get home," Daniel sighed as he stretched his arms over his head.

"Aw, come on, Pa," Joshua teased. "We've only been gone a week and a half."

Daniel laughed. "And we still have over half a week left before we will get home."

"Heya, Boss?"

Daniel turned around. "What do you need, Peter?"

"Just thought I'd let ya know thet the horses are all settled in for the night."

Daniel took a quick look around. "Thanks, Peter. Are William, Wyatt, and Flynn staying with the herd?"

"Wyatt and Flynn'll be with the herd. Will said he'd take the second turn with me." Peter gave Joshua a wink. "Ya want me to rustle up some wood fer a fire?"

Joshua stepped to the side. "Too late, Pete. I already beat you to it."

Peter shook his head with a half grin, half grimace. "You little whippersnapper, you."

Joshua grinned from ear to ear and exchanged a glance with his pa.

William rode up. "Anything else you need done, Mr. Brookings?"

"Just 'light from your horse and help Joshua get some food rustled together."

"Yes, Sir."

Later that evening, Peter, William, Joshua, and Daniel sat around the fire exchanging stories. They'd been on the trail together for three days, but had had little chance to get to know each other.

"...You could've pushed me over with a hummin'bird feather, I was so surprised." Peter chuckled. "Yessiree, that there little lady sure did have a way with words."

Leaning back on his elbows, William looked up at the stars above them. "You ever wonder how this world got its start? Where the stars came from?"

Joshua looked up at the sky and then over at William. He lay back, hands clasped under his head. "No, I don't wonder. I know where they came from."

William started. "What? How do you know that?"

Joshua gave a quick laugh and focused his eyes on one of the stars. "God told us in the Bible. 'In the beginning, God created the heavens and the earth.' And then there is the verse in one of my favorite Psalms, Psalm 19. 'The heavens declare the glory of God; and the firmament sheweth his handywork.' God made all of this. Everything. Every minor little detail of every living and non-living thing on earth and in the heavens."

William was quiet for so long that Joshua began to wonder if he had even heard.

Peter was the first to break the silence. "You guys religious?"

Joshua saw his pa's head shake in dissent. "No, we're not. We're Christians who aren't afraid to speak about our faith. But, Christianity is much more than a 'religion.'"

William sat up and stared across the fire at Daniel. "What do you mean by that?"

Joshua sat up, pulled a long blade of grass, and stuck it in his mouth. "Christianity is about a relationship with Jesus Christ, not a list of rules you have to keep to get to heaven."

Peter stood up. "William, I think it's about time for us to spell Wyatt and Flynn."

Joshua heard William sigh. "Yeah, I suppose it is."

Before William could stand up, Joshua put a hand on his shoulder. "If you ever want to talk more about the differences between religion and Christianity, just ask me, my pa, my sister, or my ma. We'd be happy to talk to you."

William nodded before heading out with Peter.

Joshua was the first to spot the house. He rode at the front of the herd and when he saw the house, he swung his hat above his head and let out a loud whoop. Ruth heard the holler and ran out of the house to greet them.

Joshua reined his horse in and leaped off to give his sister a hug. "We've got two stallions and ten mares to get us started. We also have four hands with us and two more coming in a few months with more horses."

Ruth watched the group heading toward them. "They look like good horses. What about the men?"

"Pa picked 'em out himself. He questioned them carefully before hiring them. From what I could tell on the trail, they're good men. William is a year or two older than me, but knows a lot about horses, cattle, and ranch work. He's quiet, thoughtful, and well mannered.

"Peter is the oldest of the group. He's a hardened, grizzled man with plenty of experience and a quick wit. He looks older than he acts. I'm not really sure how old he is and he won't tell me." Joshua said this last bit under his breath and behind his hand. Ruth giggled.

Joshua looked at the men again. "Let's see. Oh, yes. Wyatt and Flynn. They always seem to be paired together. They're brothers and work well together. They work hard and do as they are told, no questions asked. At least not yet. We hope they will ask questions if they don't understand something or think what we're doing won't work.

"All in all, they're all a bit rough around the edges, but what man who's lived out West for long wouldn't be?"

Ruth laughed. "Especially without a wife, mother, or sister to help them." Her eyes twinkled as she teased her brother.

"Exactly!"

After the horses were corralled, Ruth and Harriet went out to meet the new hands. They were all perfect gentlemen around Ruth and Harriet. Ruth took an immediate liking to William, though she wasn't sure why.

Peter showed Harriet some of his wit. "Too bad yer already married, Ma'am, or I'd marry you m'self."

And Harriet gave as good as she got. "Well then, I'm glad I'm already married." Her smile told him that she was teasing him and they all had a good chuckle.

Flynn and Wyatt were restless just standing around chatting and seemed glad when they were all sent off to the bunkhouse to get their beds and belongings in order.

Daniel and Joshua followed Ruth and Harriet into the house, talking nonstop about their successful trip.

Daniel left his most exciting tidbit of news to conclude with. "We even talked to an army commander from Fort Ellis. He said he would keep our ranch in mind if he ever needed more horses. We talked after we had bought this breeding stock, so he knew what quality of horses we want to breed. He seemed impressed."

"That is very good, Dear," Harriet said, smiling at him. "I am so happy that your dream is finally starting to come true."

OCTOBER 1876
DOUBLE B RANCH
As the weeks and months sped by, the ranch hands became part of the family. Wyatt and Flynn even seemed to relax some. Since there were only four ranch hands, Harriet insisted that the hands eat with the family for meals.

"It's just as easy to feed eight as it is to feed four," she exclaimed. "Eating with a family will be good for them."

Daniel gave up on arguing with his wife about the subject. Instead, he chose to truly make them all a part of the family and insisted that they join the family for devotions after dinner.

Even though Christmas was still a few months away, Daniel felt a burden to share the Christmas story a little earlier than he had planned. After the table was cleared, Daniel opened his Bible to Luke chapter two and began to read.

"'In those days, Caesar Augustus...'"

Ruth smiled at these words and listened in rapture to her father's deep, expressive voice. She felt like she lived in the story. This happened nearly every year, but this year was the first time she really put herself in Mary's place. She felt the confusion, the fear, the pain, the rejection. What would it have been like to be the mother of the Son of God? Would she have been as willing as Mary was?

God, she prayed as her father continued reading, *make me a willing maidservant for You. Help me do what You ask when You ask me to do it.*

As she prayed, a peaceful contentedness swept over her features. After her prayer, Ruth looked around the table and watched as the men listened to her father read. She noticed a tear slide down William's weather-beaten cheek, skirting his mustache before falling onto his shirt. The looks on the other men's faces were softer than she had noticed them being before. Ruth wasn't sure what word would be best to describe the look. Peaceful? No, not quite. Serene? She shook her head. No, definitely not that. Tranquil. Yes, that was it. They all had tranquil looks on their faces. As if, for this one moment in time, something was right in their lives.

Her father finished reading the Christmas story and finished up with a Scripture passage he traditionally read on Christmas Day. "'And the four beasts had each of them six wings about him; and they were full of eyes within: and they rest not day and night, saying, Holy, holy, holy, Lord God Almighty, which was, and is, and is to come.

"'And when those beasts give glory and honour and thanks to him that sat on the throne, who liveth for ever and ever, The four and twenty elders fall down before him that sat on the throne, and worship him that liveth for ever and ever, and cast their crowns before the throne, saying, Thou art worthy, O Lord, to receive glory and honour and power: for thou hast created all things, and for thy pleasure they are and were created...

"'And I beheld, and I heard the voice of many angels round about the throne and the beasts and the elders: and the number of them was ten thousand times ten thousand, and thousands of thousands;

Saying with a loud voice, Worthy is the Lamb that was slain to receive power, and riches, and wisdom, and strength, and honour, and glory, and blessing.

"'And every creature which is in heaven, and on the earth, and under the earth, and such as are in the sea, and all that are in them, heard I saying, Blessing, and honour, and glory, and power, be unto him that sitteth upon the throne, and unto the Lamb for ever and ever. And the four beasts said, Amen. And the four and twenty elders fell down and worshipped him that liveth for ever and ever.'" Daniel paused. "Let's bow our heads and silently worship our Savior." He bowed his head and the others followed his example.

Ruth bowed her head and praised God for sending His Son into the world as a baby to be her atonement for sin. Silent tears rolled down her cheeks as she considered how unworthy she was and how grateful she was that He still forgave her.

A rough hand on her shoulder made her jump. William stood next to her. "Sorry to disturb you, Miss Ruth," he whispered, "but I was wonderin' if I could ask you a few questions."

Ruth's eyes widened in confusion. "Me? Why me?"

William shrugged and he licked his lips in what seemed to be nervous agitation. "I watched you while Mr. Brookings read. I think you'll be the best one to answer my questions."

Ruth nodded, stood up, and went to where her father sat. She leaned her mouth to his ear. "Pa, Will has a few questions. Is it all right if I bring him out on the porch so we can talk?"

Daniel glanced over at William before nodding his assent.

Ruth motioned for William to follow her as she took her shawl off the hook near the door. William grabbed his coat and shrugged into it before holding the door for her to step onto the porch.

Ruth sat on the step while William leaned against one of the posts. They stared at the snow-covered mountains in the distance for a few minutes.

William finally broke the silence. "Your whole family seems to have a...somethin' different about you." He cleared his throat. "What...what's so different?"

Ruth looked up at the stars. "We all have a personal relationship with our Savior, Jesus Christ." Her eyes wandered to William's face as he looked across at the land before him.

He nodded. "Your brother explained some about that on the trail here. I know some about Jesus, but I never heard the Christmas story the way I heard it tonight. Your pa read it as if it were real to him."

"It is."

"I realize that now." He looked down at Ruth, then back out at the landscape. "I just never made the connection between Jesus' birth and the

182

celebration and worship, and then to move to the future celebration and worship... Was that part about the last times? When the world ends?" William's words trailed off.

Ruth smiled and nodded. "About the elders bowing down in worship? Yes. As for the connection between the two, Pa has a tradition of doing that. Sometimes he adds the middle part of the story."

William's eyes darted toward Ruth in surprise. "The middle?"

"Yes." Ruth's answer was soft as her mind raced, and prayed, for the words to say. "The part where Jesus gave Himself up to die for your sins and for mine. There was no celebration in heaven then. No one worshiped Him. He was forsaken and alone, but He knew what He had to do and He went into it willingly."

"Why'd He do that?" William asked.

Ruth took a deep breath as she stared unseeing at the barn. "To save you from your sins. Romans 6:23 says, 'For the wages of sin is death.' Three chapters earlier, in Romans 3:23, God states that 'all have sinned and fall short of the glory of God.' Jesus died to take away the wages of sin and restore us to the glory of God."

"He did that for me?" William looked incredulous.

Ruth stood up and faced him. "Yes. Jesus Christ, the Son of God, came as a baby to be born in a humble stable. He was worshiped by Magi, shepherds, old men, and old women. He was born to a carpenter and his virgin wife. He grew up as a normal child, though without sin. He ministered to His people, knowing they would ultimately reject Him. He died to save all mankind from their sins, but He also knew that if there had been only one man alive on earth to save, He would have died for him. He rose on the third day, defeating death and the grave. After appearing to many of His disciples and their friends, He ascended into heaven and will return again to earth someday to again be worshiped and adored as He deserves."

William listened to Ruth's passionate summary attentively. He stood in silent thought for a couple of minutes. "How does one have a personal relationship with this Jesus?"

Ruth's smile widened. "Let's go inside and let Pa tell you. He is much better than I am."

William stopped her before she reached the door. "Before we do, I was wonderin'. What were you thinking about while he was reading?"

Ruth blushed. "What it would have been like to be Mary."

William nodded. "What else?"

Ruth looked down and scuffed the toe of her boot on the planks. "How tranquil you and the other men looked while Pa was reading."

"Tranquil?" His voice held a tone of curiosity.

Ruth laughed a little and looked up at him. "Yes, tranquil. Calm, unworried, unharried."

William smiled. "That describes what I was feelin' then, too. Though a bit sad for Joseph's pain and worry, too."

Ruth nodded as a grin spread on her face. "You are very observant. Many people don't think about Joseph's side of the story. I'm glad you could have a few minutes of feeling tranquil. Now, let's get inside so Pa can answer the rest of your questions."

William held the door open for Ruth and she went straight to her father with a huge grin on her face.

"Pa, William wants to know how to get saved."

Daniel Brookings looked at the shy young man standing nervously near the door. Daniel smiled and beckoned for William to come closer while Ruth gave her mother a hug before sitting down. William took a hesitant step forward and sank into the empty chair next to Daniel.

"Ruth tells me you would like to know how to be saved."

William nodded. "Yes, Sir."

Daniel kept his eyes trained on William, but through his peripheral vision, he could tell that the other ranch hands were listening close. *Lord, give me the words to say and give William the understanding he needs.*

"William, do you believe that Jesus Christ is the Son of God?" Daniel asked.

William's hands twisted together in his lap while he thought. A few seconds ticked by before he looked up into Daniel's eyes. "Yes, Sir."

Daniel nodded. "In Acts, when Paul and Silas were asked, 'What must I do to be saved?' their response was, 'Believe on the Lord Jesus Christ, and thou shalt be saved, and thy house. And they spake unto him the word of the Lord, and to all that were in his house.'"

William blinked his eyes in obvious confusion. "That's all? Just believe?"

Daniel smiled. "Earlier in Acts, Peter told the crowds he was preaching to: 'Repent, and be baptized every one of you in the name of Jesus Christ for the remission of sins, and ye shall receive the gift of the Holy Ghost.'

"Repentance means turning completely from your sins. If you believe that Jesus Christ is the Son of God, that He died for your sins to give you the free gift of eternal life, and you feel convicted of your sins, you are one step closer to being saved. At this point, you have two directions you can go. One, you can ignore God's conviction and keep living in your sin. Or two, you can turn to Him, confess your sins, repent of your sins, and 'go, sin no more.'"

William looked like he was about to interrupt, but Daniel raised a hand for silence. "Now, I do want to clarify one thing before I go on. This does not mean you will be sinless. You will still sin, you will still have problems, but you will also have Jesus Christ, God the Father, and God the Holy Spirit in you helping you as often as you need the help and ask for it."

William stared at his hands for a few seconds before looking up at Daniel with deep conviction in his eyes. "I want that for myself," he said in a husky voice. "I need that."

Daniel put his hand on William's shoulder and looked him straight in the eye. "All you have to do is lay your heart before Jesus' feet. Talk to Him and tell Him what you want."

"I don't know where to start," William said, his voice almost a whisper.

Daniel nodded. "Lord, I come before You today with my friend William. I've told You about him before, but today he wants to talk to You for himself. Go ahead, William."

William cleared his throat. "Hi, God. I'm William. I don't really know what to say. Mr. Brookings said to just tell you what's on my heart. I've sinned a lot. Maybe nothing big like murder, but I've lied, cheated others, and lots of other things I know I shouldn't have done. I wanna stop it, God. Please come into my heart and help me to stop sinning and to live like You did when Jesus came to earth. I'm gonna need lots of help, though, just so

You know. It's not gonna be easy for either of us. Thanks for coming to die for me, Jesus. I really appreciate it. More than I could ever say."

"Amen."

CHAPTER SEVENTEEN

JANUARY 1877

CARTERSVILLE, MONTANA TERRITORY

During the long winter months, there was little to do around the ranch. Because of this, Joshua decided to spend some time in town getting to know people and learning how the city was run. He talked to the leading men in town and even offered some ideas about town development. Joshua found himself spending more and more time with one man in particular.

Sheriff Leland was an agreeable man and seemed to have taken an immediate liking to Joshua. From what Joshua could tell, the sheriff was about five years older than Joshua's brother, Matthew. Neil Leland's easy manners and Joshua's openness made for a quick and lasting friendship to form between the two.

In early February, Joshua rode into town and swung off his horse in front of the sheriff's office.

"Howdy, Joshua," the sheriff greeted him.

Joshua looked past Poseidon's head and saw Sheriff Leland sitting on the bench outside his office. "Howdy, Sheriff. How are things in town today?"

"Not too bad. It's been quiet 'round here lately." He stroked his beard. "Though not too quiet. You know..." His eyes shifted past Joshua and narrowed.

Joshua turned to see what the sheriff had seen and noticed two men facing each other near the saloon. A quick glance toward the sheriff told him that Sheriff Leland had also seen them. Sheriff Leland bolted from the bench and rushed across the street.

Joshua watched for a few seconds before walking across the street. He did not like the looks the men were giving each other and Joshua wanted to be in a position to help the sheriff if needed.

"Howdy!" Sheriff Leland hailed the two men. "Is there a problem here?"

The dark cowboy glared at the sheriff. "Nothin' for you to worry 'bout, Sheriff."

The short man glanced at the sheriff with panic on his face. Joshua saw the look and sent a quick prayer heavenward. *God, help Sheriff Leland take care of this peacefully.* He moved into position to the sheriff's right and behind the dark cowboy. Joshua noticed Sheriff Leland's eyes flicker toward him and Joshua gave him a slight nod.

Sheriff Leland addressed the dark man. "I don't believe I've ever seen you in town before."

The man sneered. "No, you ain't. And you ain't 'bout to run me out neither."

The short man jumped into the conversation. "He tried to take advantage of me. He deserves to be—"

"Shut yer mouth!" the dark man demanded. "Or I'll shut it for you." His voice laced with an intense anger that made Joshua's blood run cold.

Joshua breathed another prayer and moved in a little closer, trying to get in the best position to help ease the situation.

The sheriff swallowed hard. "I'm going to have to bring you both to the sheriff's office with me so we can get this straightened out without innocent bystanders getting hurt. If you two would kindly come with me."

"No, thank you," the dark man said with mock politeness, "I'd rather not."

Joshua saw his moment and moved quickly. Before either man could think, he was between the two men, his pistol pointed at the dark man. "You heard the sheriff, Mister. Now get moving." Joshua was surprised at how calm his voice sounded despite the thudding in his heart and the sweat on his hands.

"Who're you?" The dark man glared at Joshua.

Joshua's brain wasn't working fast enough to come up with a good response. Luckily for him, Sheriff Leland's brain was. "He's my new deputy. He just hasn't gotten his badge yet."

Joshua admired the sheriff's quick thinking. As he helped urge the two men to the sheriff's office, he wondered how much truth there might be behind the excuse. *Could Sheriff Leland be considering asking for a deputy to help him?*

After the matter between the two men was settled, the dark man was put into a jail cell for extortion, disturbing the peace, and resisting arrest. The short man was allowed to go back to his home. Joshua poured himself a cup of coffee and sat down in the chair across from the sheriff.

"Did you mean what you said about me being your deputy?"

The sheriff rubbed his beard. "I have been thinking about getting a deputy. I'm not as young as I once was and I have been thinking of doing something less wearing on the old body sometime in the near future. I'd like the next sheriff to have some training I wish I'd had. I was wrackin' my brain for who I could ask when you came in and watched my back just when I needed it most. And you did a right good job of it, too. I'd say the job's yours if you'll take it."

Joshua pondered the offer. "First of all, you are not that old. What are you, thirty?"

Sheriff Leland nodded. "Something like that. Out here in the West, though, thirty is rather old. Not to mention that my wife would like me to be around more often. And then there's the simple fact that being a sheriff is dangerous and I'd like to live to see my fortieth birthday."

Joshua smiled and shook his head. "That's true, I suppose. Well, I'll have to talk to my family about the job offer. I would like to say yes, but Pa might need me at the ranch more than I think he might."

Sheriff Leland nodded. "Understandable. Your family should always come first. Let me know when you can. I'm not in a big hurry."

Joshua nodded his thanks and stood up to leave. "I'm just glad I came into town when I did."

"So am I, Joshua. So am I."

When he got back home, Joshua talked to his family and they were all supportive of him taking the job. His father assured him that with six ranch hands, he wouldn't need Joshua's help all the time. Joshua prayed, fervently asking for God's guidance.

Less than a week later, Joshua rode into town again, this time to accept the deputy position.

MAY 1877

A few months later, Sheriff Leland sighed and put a piece of paper on the desk.

"What is it?" Joshua asked.

The sheriff rubbed his forehead in nervous agitation. "We need to take Skip and Tye to Helena."

Joshua's head jerked up from his coffee cup, a startled look on his face. "Why?"

Sheriff Leland shrugged. "The Marshal decided he wanted them there instead. So we get to take them in."

"Just the two of us?" Joshua protested. "You know they're going to have gang members watching for a chance to help them escape."

"I know that. And yes, it can only be the two of us. The men around here don't have the time to become temporary deputies and be gone for that long."

Joshua brooded as he nursed his coffee cup. Skip and Tye were members of a notorious gang of outlaws. Sheriff Leland had been lucky when he had found them. Skip and Tye had been alone and weaponless. It had been an easy capture, but not one either Joshua or Sheriff Leland wanted to repeat. "When do we leave?"

"Hopefully when the gang least expects it." Neil Leland gave a rueful smile. "Tomorrow really early in the morning sound good to you?"

Joshua nodded. "That should work. Let's leave just before sunrise."

"Can you watch the jail for a while? I'm gonna go talk to my wife."

"Take as long as you need, Sheriff. I'll be fine here."

An hour before sunrise, Joshua, Sheriff Leland, and their two prisoners left in the darkness before dawn. They traveled at a steady trot with Sheriff Leland leading and Joshua taking up the rear. Joshua and the sheriff kept a watchful and wary eye out for any hint of trouble. Nothing happened on the first day of travel.

As the terrain changed on the second day out, Joshua got nervous. More and more rocks were scattered along the road they were traveling, which meant more hiding places. He glanced up at the sky. The sun shone directly overhead. Joshua breathed a quick prayer of protection.

Joshua saw Sheriff Leland fall before he heard the gunshot. He got his rifle swiftly into position and fired at a flash of sunlight. He heard a man scream in pain as he continued looking for more attackers. The attackers kept their gun barrels in plain sight, making Joshua's job much easier. With the sun directly overhead, sunlight glinted off the gun barrels, giving Joshua the targets he needed. Joshua wondered at their stupidity, but thanked God for it at the same time.

Out of the corner of his eye, he saw the prisoners' horses skitter about. But he put them out of his mind knowing that they were pretty well trapped between the sheriff's horse, the rocks, and his horse. *God help me,* he thought as he aimed at another rifle barrel. Leaning low against Poseidon's neck, he thanked his pa for training this horse to not be skittish around gunfire.

Joshua winced as a bullet whistled past his ear. He squeezed off another shot, then another, and another. He stayed hunkered down until he was sure that no more shots would be fired.

Joshua tied the prisoners' horses to the sheriff's horse and told the horse to stay. Knowing that Sheriff Leland had trained his horse to take orders, he felt safe to leave the prisoners alone for a few minutes.

He rode a quick circle around the rocks making sure all the outlaws were either wounded or killed. Then, and only then, did he approach the sheriff's motionless body. As soon as he was close enough to see the wound, all of Joshua's hopes died. His only consolation was that the sheriff had died right away.

Joshua draped the sheriff's body over the dead man's horse and led the horse behind him, with the prisoners' horses tied to Sheriff Leland's horse. As he rode, neither he nor his prisoners said a word. Joshua tried not to think about Sheriff Leland or his wife. The grief was too much to bear until his journey was complete.

Joshua pushed on through the night and they reached Helena early in the morning. He handed the prisoners over to the Marshal and then brought the body to the coroner. He asked for a coffin and buckboard to carry the body back.

Once his business was taken care of, Joshua ate a quick meal and picked up the body before riding out for home. He drove until nightfall, slept fitfully for a few hours, and started out again a couple of hours before the sun started to rise.

Joshua kept his mind blank of all thought of the attack by keeping Scripture, hymns, and memories of his family in the forefront of his mind. By pushing himself and the two horses to the max, he rode into town just over a day after Sheriff Leland had been shot.

Driving straight to the coroner's office, he got help bringing the coffin in, barely saying a word to the stunned man. The coroner got a few words out of Joshua, but only just enough to know that the sheriff had been shot and needed to be ready to be buried the next morning.

Joshua left the coroner's office and trudged to the Leland residence. He hesitated before knocking on the door.

The door opened and Mrs. Leland stared at Joshua. "You look exhausted, Joshua!" She looked behind him. "Where's Neil?"

Joshua held up a hand to stop her question. "May I come in and sit down, Ma'am?"

"Of course." Her voice was more hesitant and Joshua knew she was figuring things out. "Come on in. I'll get you a cup of coffee."

"No, thank you, Ma'am. I'll just say what needs saying and leave." Joshua sank into a kitchen chair and stared at his boots. "Your husband—"

"He's dead, isn't he?" Mrs. Leland whispered. Her eyes filled with tears and her lower lip trembled. "I had a feeling...I had a feeling something would happen."

"Yes, Ma'am. We were ambushed. He was in the lead and took a bullet right in the heart."

Mrs. Leland swallowed her tears. "And the prisoners?"

"In Helena under the Marshal's custody."

Mrs. Leland's lips turned up a slight smile. "You've done my husband proud, Joshua. Thank you."

Joshua nodded. "You're welcome, Ma'am. I wish—"

"God has a reason for this." She laughed hoarsely. "I don't know what, but I know He does."

Joshua looked down at the floor again. "Yes, Ma'am. I'm sure He does. I'd best be going. I'll see you tomorrow at the funeral, 'less you want me to stay?"

Mrs. Leland shook her head. "No, but perhaps you could send Ruth or your mother here?" She gave

Joshua a forced smile. "I don't want to be here alone right now."

Joshua tried to interrupt her, but she held up a hand. "Joshua, you are exhausted and need some rest. The best way you can help me right now is to get home, send your mother or sister over here, and then get some rest."

Joshua closed his eyes and took a deep breath. "Thank you, Ma'am." He turned slowly and found his way to the front door, letting himself out of the house.

Joshua allowed his horse, Poseidon, to choose his own pace on the way home. Home. That had a nice ring to it. If only he could go home and sleep for two or three days. But, no. He had a funeral to attend the next morning and he would be filling in as sheriff until a new sheriff was appointed or elected.

"Joshua!"

The voice seemed to float somewhere in his brain. Who had said it? He tried to look around, but his eyes and head would not cooperate.

"Is he hurt?" A male voice this time. Then someone touched him and he jerked awake. Ruth stood by his horse, William and his parents nearby.

William was the first to speak. "I'll take care of Poseidon, Joshua. You look beat."

"Thanks." Joshua tried to smile, but all he could do was slide his exhausted body off his horse and try to stay steady as he stood. "I am beat. I drove pretty much straight from Helena here."

Joshua looked up and saw concern on his father's face.

"Only you?" Daniel asked.

Joshua closed his eyes against the pain in his chest. Why did his new best friend have to die like that? "Yes. We were ambushed and the sheriff was killed. His funeral is first thing in the morning."

"Oh, poor Mrs. Leland. Mother?" Ruth breathed and turned to Harriet.

"Yes, Ruth, if your father is agreeable, you may go do your best to comfort the woman."

The words rang a bell in Joshua's head. "Oh, yeah, Mrs. Leland did ask if Ruth or Mother could go stay with her for a little while."

Daniel nodded his consent. As Ruth walked to the stable to saddle her horse, Joshua realized that William seemed to want to ask him something.

"What is it, William?"

"What happened? You don't seem to be hurt, and yet the sheriff is dead."

Joshua sighed. "Sheriff Leland was in the lead and I was in the rear. He took the first bullet and I shot the rest of the men." He laughed bitterly as he recalled the day. "They weren't very smart about their choices. The sun was directly overhead and glinted off their rifle barrels. After shooting 'em all, I got the prisoners to Helena."

William nodded before walking Poseidon to the barn.

"Good for you, Son." Daniel's voice was husky with emotion. "You did the right thing. Now go in and get some rest. We'll wake you in time for the funeral."

Joshua nodded his thanks and dragged himself into the house and to the bed that had been calling his name all day.

The next morning as Joshua and his family and most of their hands neared town, Joshua noticed that nearly the whole town was at the sheriff's funeral. Sheriff Leland had been a friendly and well-liked man. Joshua stood through the funeral in a daze. His mind was foggy and he had a hard time accepting that his friend and leader was gone.

After the funeral, Mrs. Leland thanked Joshua again. She was tearful, but strong. Joshua was about to go to his horse and take a long ride to clear his mind when he heard his name. He turned and saw Mayor Wilson coming his way.

"Joshua, I am glad I caught you." He paused to catch his breath. "I know this is all still hard on you, with Sheriff Leland being such a good friend and all, but we would like you to consider becoming the new sheriff."

Joshua stared at the man.

The mayor chuckled. "I know what you are thinking. 'How can they ask me that? I'm only eighteen. I've only been a deputy for nine months.' Well, stop thinking those thoughts. We all know what you are capable of. No matter how much you diminish what you did, your quick thinking and shooting kept the prisoners' rescuers at bay and you even got them to Helena. All by yourself. That, in and of itself, is quite an accomplishment. In the months you have been deputy, you have shown good tactical skills as well as a quick brain and a quick gun hand. Not many men have all of those combined. Sheriff Leland would have been honored to know you were his replacement. He had been talking a little about possibly retiring from sheriff duties and doing something else and mentioned to me just a few weeks ago that you would make a good sheriff. But, enough of my talking. What do you say?"

Joshua was honored and stunned. He didn't know what to think. Could he really be the sheriff of this town? "I will have to pray about it and talk to my family—"

"Of course, of course!" the mayor interrupted. "You do that. You can give me your answer in, say, two days?"

Joshua nodded and nearly ran to his horse. He touched his spurs to the dun and rode off at a gallop.

A long, hard ride was just what he needed to clear his mind, digest the events of the last three days, and, most important of all, pray.

CHAPTER EIGHTEEN

"Mayor Wilson?"

"Come on in, Joshua." The large man stepped around his desk. "You have your answer, I take it."

"Yes, Sir."

"Well, speak up. Do you accept the position?"

Joshua swallowed. "Yes, Sir, I accept the job of sheriff until a special election can be held."

The mayor stared at Joshua. "A special election? I hadn't thought of that. Of course! That would be splendid. You must run, of course, but this will give others a chance at the job, too."

"Why must I run?" Joshua was confused.

"You are the best man for the job, so you must run. Don't worry about it. I will handle all of the politicking for you."

Joshua scrunched his eyebrows. This man was too manipulative at times. "No. If I decide to run I'll have my sister do that for me. But, thank you for the offer." *Just because this man is the father of my sister's friend doesn't mean he has the right to run my life,* Joshua thought before quickly repenting of his bad attitude.

The mayor shot Joshua a questioning glance, but recovered with a speed indicative of a good politician. "Right. I will let you know when the election is to be held. In the meantime, Sheriff Brookings, I suggest you get on the job. If you would like to pick a temporary deputy, you may."

"The election will be held within the next month, right?"

"Yes, it will."

"I should be fine working on my own until after the election."

The mayor nodded. "Very well. Good luck to you, young man."

"Thanks."

Joshua's first full day on the job turned out to be exciting. The night before, two strangers had come to town and heard about the new sheriff. One of the men fancied himself to be a fast gunman and always tried to pick a fight.

After Joshua had opened up the sheriff's office for the day, Carl, a young boy from town, came into the office.

"What is it, Carl?"

"Just thought I'd warn you, Sir. There's a man who came into town looking for a fight. My pa says he's a mean 'un."

Joshua smiled. "Thank you, Carl. I'll look into it."

Joshua followed Carl out the door just in time to see Annabelle walk out of the dress shop. *Dressed in another fancy dress.* He shook his head. *I don't know what Ruth sees in her as a friend. She's going to get in trouble someday.*

He turned his attention to the other side of the road and saw two men enter the saloon. *One of them must be the man looking for a fight. I've never seen them before.*

As if in response to his thoughts, Carl pointed across the street. "That's the two men walkin' into the saloon."

Joshua nodded his thanks to Carl before he walked into the saloon. He looked through the smoky haze to find the two new men. Spotting them at the bar, he walked over to talk with them.

"Mornin'. I'm the sheriff in town. I heard you two were new here and just wanted to introduce myself. I'm Sheriff Brookings. I help keep law and order in town, so I would appreciate it if you two would keep those guns in your belts and not use them while you are here." He watched their response from the corner of his eyes.

The husky man visibly tensed at Joshua's words. *He's likely never been spoken to like that before,* Joshua mused. The wiry man kept staring at his glass with a sneer on his face.

"We'll see what we can do about that," the husky man said.

Joshua looked at the two men and got the distinct impression that he would end up dealing with both of them today. He started to walk out of the saloon.

"Hey, Sheriff! Why don't you want us to use our guns in town? Are you a coward? Don't you think you can beat me in a draw?"

Joshua ignored the man and kept walking. He heard a stool scrape the floor and footsteps hurrying toward him. A hand grabbed his arm and spun him around.

"I'm talkin' to you, Sheriff." The last word was spit out of his mouth as if it had disgusted the man. "When I'm talkin', I don't like bein' ignored."

Joshua stared coolly into the large man's face. "I noticed," he said.

The large man glared at Joshua. "I called you a coward."

"I know. I don't think you believe it though."

The large man let go of Joshua and swung his right fist at Joshua's face. Joshua ducked under the punch and strode for the door. He had a good idea what they planned next and wanted it to happen

208

outside on the quiet street where fewer people could be hurt.

Joshua walked with deliberation until he got to the sheriff's office. He turned around. The man hadn't followed him. *Maybe there won't be trouble after all. Or maybe he just decided to let me stew on his words awhile.* Joshua sat on the bench outside the office. He prayed there would be no trouble, but would not count on it. When it broke loose, he wanted to be there.

Half an hour later, the two men left the saloon and were walking down the street. Joshua watched them with wary eyes. He was the first to see the young woman step out of her house and walk down the street toward the two men.

Joshua stood up, knowing something bad was about to happen. He had to get to Annabelle before the two men saw her and accosted her. Joshua grimaced when he saw the leering look on the wiry man's face as he caught sight of Annabelle. *Dear God, let me get there in time.* He had twice the distance the other men had. He knew running would just set them off even more.

Joshua strode across the street and down the boardwalk. He kept a close eye on the two men walking toward Annabelle. Annabelle seemed oblivious to the danger until her head went up and she saw the two strangers leering at her. She tried to turn around, but it was too late; the men had already reached her.

The large man crossed the road and left the wiry man alone with Annabelle. Joshua breathed a prayer of relief. At least he would only have to take care of one of them at a time. The wiry man grabbed Annabelle's arm and talked quietly to her while she struggled to get away.

Joshua drew his revolver and cocked the hammer.

"Let me go, you brute!" Annabelle protested.

Joshua's voice came hard and unrelenting. "The lady asked you to leave her alone."

The wiry man sneered at Joshua. "What can a boy like you do? You probably don't even know any of the laws."

Joshua's eyes hardened in their resolve. "You are under arrest, Mister."

"For what?"

"Assaulting a young lady, disturbing the peace, and resisting arrest." By this time, Joshua stood next to Annabelle, his gun pointed at the wiry man's chest. "Let her go," he demanded through clenched teeth. "And put your hands on top of your head."

"And if I don't let go of her?" the wiry man asked.

"I will put a bullet into your arm."

The wiry man let go of Annabelle. He left his hands dangling by his sides and glared at Joshua.

Joshua took a step closer, keeping his eyes on the man. "Hands above your head, Mister."

The wiry man continued to stare into Joshua's eyes in a silent challenge.

Without taking his eyes off the man, Joshua spoke in a low, menacing voice. "You are begging for a bullet to the arm, aren't you?"

A cocky grin formed on the wiry man's face. "Nope, I'm not. I just don't think you can do it."

Joshua was tempted to close his eyes in frustration, but resisted the temptation knowing it could be fatal. He kept his breath steady and watched the man carefully. His timing would have to be perfect.

Seeing his opening, Joshua flipped his gun around and pistol-whipped the man in the head. The wiry man dropped to the ground and Joshua turned to Annabelle.

"Are you okay?"

Annabelle's breath came in short gasps. "Yes, I am fine, thanks to you." Tears sprang to her eyes. "I don't know what would have happened if you hadn't been here."

"I'm just glad you're okay," Joshua said.

Annabelle lowered her eyes. "Thank you, Joshua."

Joshua nodded before turning his attention to the man on the ground. He grabbed the man by the shoulders and dragged him across the street to the jail.

After locking the jail cell and stepping back outside to watch for trouble from the other man, he saw Annabelle heading his way. *God, do You really have to let her come here today? Like my day wasn't already bad enough? You know her and I get along about as well as two tomcats laying claim to the same place. How her and Ruth ever became friends, I'll never understand. And now she has an infernal infatuation with me?* He took a deep breath to steady himself.

"Joshua," Annabelle said in her airy voice, "I just had to come over and thank you more appropriately. You were distracted by that horrible man and I was still recovering from the shock. Thank you so much for saving me from that man. He was a despicable brute. What man would do that?"

Joshua bit his tongue. *Do I dare say what I really want to say? No, it isn't my place. Maybe I can talk to Ruth and have her say something.* "I was just doing my job, Annabelle—"

"Yes, I know that, but you did it so—"

Joshua held his hand up to silence her. He stared at the man approaching them. "Annabelle, I suggest you go inside the dress shop right now."

Annabelle's already dark eyes darkened. "Why?"

"The other man is coming this way. I think he is after me. I don't want you to get caught in the middle." Joshua stared hard into her face. "Go, now!"

Annabelle's frightened eyes turned toward the other man before she ran to the dress shop next to the sheriff's office.

Joshua breathed a sigh of relief and turned to go into his office.

"Sheriff!" a deep, angry voice yelled.

Joshua ignored him and put his hand on the doorknob. A bullet whipped past his shoulder as he pushed the door open. Joshua turned to face the man.

"I purposely missed. I wasn't about to shoot a man in the back."

"What do you want?" Joshua growled.

"I want my partner out of your jail."

"Not happening. He assaulted a young lady and resisted arrest. He will stay in the jail for two weeks and pay a fine."

The husky man glared at Joshua. "I want you dead," he said in a quiet, menacing voice. "I want you deader'n the men up in Boot Hill. I want you deader'n the wood in the door."

Joshua drew his breath in through his clenched teeth. "Why do you hate me so much?"

"You're the law here. I hate all laws and lawmakers and law enforcers. My goal is to get rid of 'em all."

Joshua chuckled. "Good luck with that."

"Are you ready to draw?"

Joshua did not answer; he walked out into the middle of the street, scanning the boardwalks. No one was out today. Good. "I'm ready when you are," he stated. *Dear God, help me teach this man a lesson without getting myself killed.*

The large man stepped into the middle of the street and crouched into a gunman's stance, his hands ready to draw. Joshua watched the man's eyes.

Both men drew at the same time. The large man's gun flashed first, but his bullet went wide of its mark. Joshua's gun flashed just seconds later, hitting the man's gun hand.

Joshua's opponent dropped his gun and hollered in pain, grabbing his hand. Joshua walked over to the injured man, unbuckled his gun belt, and picked up his gun. "The doc's office is two doors down. When you're ready to leave town, come by my office and I'll tell you where I hid your belt and guns."

Joshua turned his back and walked into his open office door. He prayed he had made the right decision to leave that man alive. He hated to kill a man. Maiming someone's dominant hand for life was hard to do, but he hoped the man would one day come to appreciate his second chance at life. Maybe it would even make him think about his way of life.

CHAPTER NINETEEN

MAY 1877

WYOMING TERRITORY

Jed scanned the herd for the millionth time. It had been only two days, but he was already exhausted. Herding a hundred and fifty cattle with just three cowpokes to keep them in line was harder than he had originally thought. When they had talked about taking the cattle to Cheyenne, Walter had raised the question and Jed had rejected it. Now he was regretting his decision to rustle so many cattle at once before moving them to Cheyenne.

"Charles!" Jed yelled.

Jed breathed a sigh of relief as Charles looked toward the cattle nearest him, saw the problem, and moved the three stubborn cattle back into the herd.

Jed turned to see Walter riding up to him. "What is it, Walter?"

"We stoppin' soon?"

Jed looked up at the sky. It was getting on toward dark. "Yeah. How 'bout you scout ahead for a good camp?"

Walter nodded and rode off.

That night, as Jed took his turn watching the herd, he let his mind wander. When Jed realized that he was only a day's ride from Cheyenne, he jumped off his horse and led it around the sleeping herd. His teeth gritted together and his muscles were wound up tighter than the densest thorn patch.

"What am I doin' here?" Jed mumbled. "Why didn't we go somewhere else?" He rolled his eyes. "Yeah, like we would've ever made it to Abilene or anywhere else. Cheyenne was the closest place to go and Walter and Charles would've thought I was crazy not to go there." He paused in his nervous pacing and looked up at the stars.

As the gentle lowing of the cattle reached his ears, Jed's agitated nerves began to relax and he mounted his horse to make a circuit around the herd.

The cattle were still quiet when Walter took over for Jed. Jed rolled out his bedroll and lay down. As tired as he was, his mind would not be still. Every time he closed his eyes, the girl's face would pop into his head. The fear in her eyes, the whimpers, the cries. Jed threw back the blanket with a violence that came close to putting out the small fire. He sat up, his fists clenched, and hissed through his teeth, "You will not torture me like this, Elizabeth. I won't allow it! I was outta my head."

"You okay, Jed?" Charles's sleepy voice penetrated Jed's foggy thoughts.

Jed cleared his throat. "Yeah, I'm fine. Just having trouble getting to sleep. Too tired." *And tortured by the worst mistake I ever made.*

Charles must have been satisfied with Jed's answer. Jed heard him roll over and soon his snores could be heard. Jed eased himself back down to his bedroll and tried to keep his mind clear of everything.

The next thing Jed knew, he was being prodded by the toe of someone's boot. He groaned.

"I think he might be alive, Walter."

Jed felt someone leaning over him. "You might be right, Charles, but we've been known to be wrong afore."

Jed whipped his pistols out of their holsters and pointed one at each of the brothers. "Get outta here!" he growled.

Walter raised an eyebrow. "Okay, we were just trying to wake you up before the day—"

"I don't care," Jed said, a scowl on his face. "Get!"

Charles backed away, but didn't leave. "Does this have somethin' to do with the Elizabeth character you were talkin' about last night?"

Jed's eyes narrowed dangerously and he kept them focused on Charles. "If you wanna live past the mornin', I suggest you get outta my sight right now."

Jed was pleased to see the fear enter Charles's eyes and watched him beat a hasty retreat. Once the brothers were out of his sight, Jed holstered his pistols and packed his camp gear. Once he had them loaded onto his horse, he doused the fire and mounted up.

"All right, cowboys! Let's get rolling!"

The sun was setting when they arrived outside Cheyenne. After three days spent eating dust, drinking small amounts of water, and herding cattle in a westerly direction, they were all glad to see the town. Even Jed. Walter and Charles stayed with the cattle while Jed went into town to find someone to buy the cattle.

Jed was on edge all the next day as he searched for a buyer, but he finally found one, sold the cattle, and got the money. There had been one anxious moment when the buyer looked a little too carefully at one of the brands, but he didn't say anything about it.

After the cattle were sold, Jed breathed a sigh of relief and split the money between them. "Don't spend it all in one place," he said with a wink. He was nervous about spending any more time in Cheyenne, but also knew that it was very unlikely that Elizabeth would see him or that he would see her.

Charles and Walter laughed and walked to the saloons. Jed looked up and down the street. *That place'll do. All I need is a coupla beers to satisfy my thirst and then I'll be set for a while.* Two days on the town nearly depleted Charles's and Walter's money, but Jed was careful not to spend much, to stay out of sight, and to not get drunk again. He had learned from the last time he had been in Cheyenne.

Jed was annoyed that it had taken him two days to convince his partners to leave Cheyenne. All three of them knew that Charles and Walter had their faces on wanted posters from previous crimes. But did they think of that? Of course not!

They needed to leave and find a new outfit set up for rustling. Jed was tempted to find a cold mountain spring and dump the two brothers into it. Maybe that would wake them from their drunken stupor. Instead, he just led them away and searched for a new area to rustle cattle and horses from.

There were plenty of ranches in the west and they continued to pilfer a few cattle from each ranch until they had another hundred cattle to sell.

After selling the cattle from their second batch, Jed heard about someone who needed a hired gunman. It would only take a couple of weeks, so he talked to the man and took the job. Walter and Charles chose to lie low and try not to make trouble.

Jed rode steadily southward to Beloit, Kansas, a small town northwest of Abilene. The man who hired him on needed to get to Abilene and had hired Jed to keep him safe. From whom Jed didn't know yet.

It took Jed three and a half uneventful days to get from northern Wyoming to the middle of Kansas and he was glad to see the sign announcing the town of Beloit. He stopped in at the saloon, put a silver dollar on the bar, and asked for a whiskey. After the bartender had poured his whiskey, Jed looked him over with a practiced eye.

"D'you know where I might find a Mr. Calvin Winters?"

"Depends on who's askin'." The man rested his elbows on the bar and stared Jed in the eye.

"He hired me on back in Wyoming."

"He ain't been to Wyoming recently."

Jed fought the grin threatening to take over his face. "We done it over telegram."

The bartender straightened and gave Jed a once-over. "Ahh, you must be the new guy he's been talkin' about." He turned to his right and hollered, "Cal! There's someone here wantin' ta see ya."

222

Jed turned around and watched as a tall, thin man turned in his seat in the back corner of the saloon. Jed caught the man's eye and they both nodded as Calvin Winters stood up and limped over to the bar.

"Jed?" The man's voice was rough and sounded like he had sandpaper in his throat.

"That's me." Jed stuck out his hand and Calvin shook it.

"You done here?"

Jed grabbed his glass and drained it before answering. "Yup."

Calvin took a quick look around the saloon before walking to the double swinging doors. Jed followed his new boss through the doors and to their horses.

They rode in silence for almost half an hour before Calvin nodded to an opening in the fence. "That's my place. We'll go to the house and talk."

Jed and Calvin dismounted in front of the white clapboard house, tied their horses to hitching posts, and walked inside. Jed stayed just inside the doorway until his eyes adjusted to the dim light. He heard Calvin shuffling around inside and when he could see more clearly, he saw papers spread across the table and Calvin staring at one in his hands.

Calvin looked up and Jed approached the table. "You ready?"

"Ready as I'll ever be, Boss."

Calvin nodded. "I'm assuming you can read," he stated. Without waiting for Jed's answer, he continued. "I've got a contract for you to sign, but we'll get to that after we talk about what I want you to do." He gestured at the chair Jed was standing behind. "Have a seat."

Jed spun the chair around so the back faced the table before swinging his leg over the chair to straddle it.

"I s'pose you want to know what you're needed for."

Jed nodded. "Yep."

"I've got five sons and one daughter. My sons all work on this ranch and my daughter lives with her husband in a house on my land. Her husband is the foreman, so I let him build." Calvin took a deep breath. "Now, I'm gettin' on in years and want my will settled afore I die. To do that, I need to get to Abilene. Abilene is the closest place with a lawyer. All my ranch hands know I'm plannin' on goin'.

"If I die without a will, the hands, my sons, and my foreman and daughter will have to fight it out as ta who gets the ranch." He gave a heavy sigh. "I was a failure of a father with all but my youngest son and my daughter. The other four are bad characters and I wouldn't be surprised if one or all of them attempted to ambush me on the way to Abilene."

Jed squinted his eyes and held up a hand. "Wait, if the bartender knew I was comin', how do your sons not know?"

"My four oldest are on a cattle drive to Lubbock, Texas, and have been for the last three weeks. They'll be gone for a while, but will ride hard once they hear where I've gone. And the barkeep doesn't know what kind of hired man you are." Calvin put his paper down and leaned across the table. "I've kept it quiet that I'm hirin' somebody. The barkeep knew you were comin' because I told him to send you out my way iffen you showed up there. My foreman also knows. Far as anyone else knows, yer just a new hand or somethin'. They'll figger it out soon enough, but not in time to do anythin'.

"Main thing I need from you is to keep my boys from killin' me on the way to Abilene. If they kill me on the way back, I need ya to get the will safely back to my daughter and youngest son. I'll be havin' three copies made. One for me to carry and two for you. No matter what happens to me you'll take your two copies back here to my son and daughter. You in?"

Jed stared at Calvin. "Depends on the money."

Calvin named an amount.

Jed raised his eyebrows. That amount was more than he'd made in two gunslingin' jobs. "I'm in."

Calvin stood up and slapped his leg. "Good. We leave bright and early in the morning. Your bedroom is up those stairs and to the right. Your horse can go in the barn. Dinner is at eight, breakfast at five."

Jed nodded as he got off the chair and headed outside to bed down his horse.

The next two days were uneventful as they started their journey to Abilene. Jed kept a careful eye for any possible ambush spots. No dust clouds showed up behind them and they took turns sleeping at night. The third day Calvin and Jed were both more nervous. The older sons had been expected back the same day the two men left and with hard riding could be waiting ahead on the trail.

Jed set the pace at a slow trot and watched the terrain as it grew more ambush-worthy.

"Calvin, I suggest you stay low in the saddle. The more you look like your horse, the better."

"Good idea."

They rode in silence again. Jed wasn't much of a talker and Calvin had run out of things to say around noon the previous day. Twenty-four hours later, Calvin and Jed were silent as church mice. And it was a good thing, too.

The silence gave Jed's hearing a boost and his ears caught the sound of a rifle hammer being pulled back just around the next curve. He reined in his horse and signaled for Calvin to stop. Calvin did so and slid off his horse, moving into the trees. Jed gave him a nod and slid off his horse, checking each hoof to give the ruse that he had stopped for other reasons. He mounted up on his horse again and rode right on through the ambush spot. Out of the corner of his eye, he saw two people on either side of the trail and made a mental note of their positions.

Once out of sight, he dismounted, tied his horse to a tree off the trail, and circled around through the trees. He found Calvin.

"You go get behind the two boys over here. I'll do the same with t'others and I'll do all the talkin'."

Calvin nodded. "I'll get it done."

Calvin locked eyes with Jed before Jed headed around to the other side of the road.

Jed stood behind the unsuspecting boys for a minute, a grin on his face. He couldn't believe these boys were Calvin's sons. These men didn't have any sense of anything in them, especially hearing.

"All right, boys," he shouted. "We've gotcha surrounded. Leave your guns where they are and stand up slowly with your hands in the air. If you don't, I will personally put a bullet in each of your heads."

Jed almost laughed out loud when he saw one of the boys nearly jump out of his skin when he first started talking. The two men in front of him dropped their guns and stood up as slowly as they could, hands raised in the air as high as they would go.

In his peripheral vision, Jed could see that the boys on the other side of the road were doing the same thing.

"Now all of you march to the middle of the road," Jed ordered. After the four men were in the middle of the road, Calvin gave a whistle and his horse trotted toward them.

Jed kept his gun trained on the men while Calvin took the coil of rope off his horse.

"Put your hands behind your backs," Jed said, and Calvin tied them all together in single file as they obeyed Jed's order.

Once they were all secure, Jed stepped in front of them and glared at them. "You'll walk where ya wanna go now. We'll take yer horses back to the ranch with us. When you get back to the ranch, you can have yer horses back." He turned his back on them and started walking to his horse.

By the time Jed was back in his saddle, Calvin had joined him.

"We're just goin' to leave 'em here?" Calvin asked.

"Yep. It's the best chance of gettin' you back to the ranch alive."

Calvin shook his head. "I'll be. I never thought it'd be that easy."

"One thing's for sure," Jed said. "Those boys don't got even the slightest lick o' sense that you've got."

Calvin laughed. "You got that right."

While in town waiting for Calvin to finish with his lawyer, Jed hung around in the saloons, still hoping that maybe—just maybe—he'd hear something about the kids.

"Hey, Mister, you heard about the kid elected sheriff in Montana?"

Jed looked up at the gruff-voiced man across the table and shook his head.

"It's all over the newspapers and town," the man said. "You wanna hear more 'bout it?"

Jed saw the twinkle in the elderly man's eyes and knew he would hear about it whether he wanted to or not. *A kid elected sheriff? This could be good. Might even be a good place to go to once I get back to camp if it's cattle territory.* "Sure," Jed said.

The elderly man eased into the chair across from him and gave a contented sigh. "Well, apparently there's this kid—he's nineteen the way I hear it—and he was the deputy for a while. They was on their way to deliver some pris'ners to Helena, the big city in Montana. Anyway, they was on their way there and got ambushed by some of the pris'ners' buddies. Sheriff got kilt, the buddies got kilt, the pris'ners and deputy got outta there alive, and the pris'ners got delivered to Helena.

"When the kid got back, the mayor asked him to be the fill-in sheriff until a special election could be held. The kid said, accordin' to the paper, that he prayed about whether to run or not and felt God tellin' him to run. The kid won in a landslide. Only one other person on the ballot. An older man, probably somewhere's between mine and your ages.

"The kid won with somethin' like seventy percent of the vote. He's the sheriff and doin' a right good job of it apparently. Wouldn't surprise me if he ran fer president one of these years."

Jed raised an eyebrow. "Why d'you say that?"

"Aw, shucks! He's got a way with his gun and his words. What more does a politician need out here?" The man bounced his white eyebrows up and down a few times.

Jed shook his head. "That'd work out here, but not in the East." He stood up. "Thanks for the story."

"Thanks fer listenin'. Not many people listen to me anymore." Jed saw a flicker of grief flash in the man's eyes before Jed walked past him and went to the bar to pay for his drink.

On his way to the hotel, Jed saw a newspaper and bought one. When he got back to his room, he flipped through it to see if there was anything about the kid sheriff. There was a short article about him. *Joshua Brookings,* Jed thought. *Yes, Joshua, we will most definitely be paying you a visit. This article confirms everything...well, most of what that old man said.* An unpleasant-looking grin spread across Jed's face. *You won't have any idea how to handle these trained outlaws, will you?* He chuckled as he folded up the newspaper and prepared to leave town.

Less than a week after leaving Abilene, Jed rode into camp with a new gleam in his eyes.

After ground-staking Copper, Jed poured himself some coffee and sat down near the fire. Charles and Walter knew better than to ask Jed anything about his trip. From the looks of the camp, Jed guessed they were more than ready to move on anyway.

"Where we goin' next?" Charles asked. "Any ideas?"

"Cartersville, Montana," Jed said.

Walter looked surprised at Jed's fast answer. "Cartersville? Never heard of it."

"It's a small town, recently built near Bozeman and Fort Ellis, and has some of the best cattle and horse country around. It also has some very good, very large cattle ranches and one excellent horse ranch." Jed's grin turned sly. "They also have a new sheriff who is only nineteen years old."

"Who elects a kid for sheriff?" Walter asked.

Jed shook his head. "That's why the news is all over the territory already. Apparently he became sheriff by default because he was the deputy when the sheriff was killed. They held an election shortly after and still voted him in despite his age. I have no idea why anyone would want a kid as their sheriff, but apparently they did. It was a landslide for the kid."

Charles's head shook in disbelief. "When do we leave?" he asked.

"Tomorrow at daybreak," Jed said.

Two weeks later, Charles, Walter, and Jed had all their supplies gathered and had a hiding place set up for the cattle and horses they intended to rustle. As usual, they each went separate directions to stake out the ranches, returning to the camp a week later to report their findings.

Charles spoke first. "The four ranches to the south and west of town will be easy. The cattle just roam free and aren't guarded well."

Jed nodded. "The five ranches to the west and north of town should be fairly easy for the same reasons. There is a horse ranch that will give us a little trouble since the horses are fenced in, but it shouldn't be too bad."

Charles and Jed looked at Walter. "I'm glad we'll have some easy ones. The ranches to the north and east of town'll be a problem. Well, not quite all of them. There are two that won't be too hard. But, the other two—"

Jed knit his eyebrows together. "Why will they be so difficult?"

"They are well guarded and fenced in," Walter replied. "One of them is a horse ranch. For obvious reasons, they want to keep a close eye on them. The other one, the cattle are rarely left alone, even at night."

"Names?" Jed asked.

"Double B and Bar 8," Walter said. "The Double B is the horse ranch and the Bar 8 is the cattle ranch."

Jed thought for a minute. "We'll leave them for the last ones we do. Maybe we can get enough without 'em."

"The Double B has the best-lookin' horses I ever did see," Walter said.

"We'll hit it last. That'll give us time to think of a way to get 'em without getting caught."

Walter smiled a little. "Thanks, Jed. I knew you'd think of somethin'. I was worried that I'd just be a voice of doom."

Jed laughed. "Naw, there's always ways around little things like guards and fences."

Two months, eighty newly acquired cattle, and twenty new horses later, Jed was worried. "The ranchers will be getting anxious now. But we can't go without at least a few more head of cattle or horses."

"Let's try the Double B," Walter suggested.

"You have a plan to get in there?" Charles asked.

"Sure, we just take part of the fence down," Walter replied.

"What about the guards?" Jed asked.

Walter slapped his hat against his thigh. "We... Surely they can't be guardin' all them horses at the same time! If we need to, we just shoot them guards. The pasture's gotta be too far away for a gunshot to be heard at the bunkhouse or the main house. Not clearly anyways."

Jed was silent for a few minutes. "That might just work," he said slowly. He paused to think. "Let's give it a try. We'll spend a coupla days scoutin' out the Double B and then we'll strike."

CHAPTER TWENTY

SEPTEMBER 1877

CARTERSVILLE, MONTANA TERRITORY

The hills were turning beautiful colors and the air began to cool. Joshua took a deep breath. He loved autumn.

"Sheriff!" a sharp voice broke into his reverie.

"Hello, Ralph. What can I do for you?"

"If you don't do something about the rustlers, we'll have to take the law into our own hands!"

Joshua sighed. "It is hard to catch rustlers when they don't post up a notice of what ranch they are going to hit next. I don't have enough men to stake out at every ranch around here."

The hot-tempered man cooled down. "I know, but my ranch just lost ten more cattle. That's thirty already this month! I can't afford to lose that many cattle."

"I'll see what I can do, Ralph."

Joshua watched Ralph leave the office with ponderous steps.

"Joshua?"

Joshua turned toward his office. "What is it, Micah?"

Micah fiddled with his deputy star. "I had an idea about the rustlers. What if we stake out your pa's place? They haven't hit there yet. I know it's got the best horses around and they've been stealing horses and cattle alike. I'm just wonderin' why they haven't gone there yet."

Joshua was thoughtful. "You have a good idea there. You watch the office. I'm going to go have a talk with my pa."

Two nights later, Micah, Joshua, and five new deputies—all the ranch hands and Daniel Brookings from the Double B Ranch—lay in wait for the rustlers. After a month of chasing down rustlers who knew how to hide their tracks well, Joshua hoped and prayed that his gamble would be right. He hoped that the rustlers would try to rustle the horses off his pa's ranch. His gamble was that they would do it tonight. And if not tonight, soon. Their herd had to be getting pretty big by now and they would have to leave soon. Joshua watched and prayed he had made the right decision.

The moon had almost slipped behind the distant hills when he saw the movement. Joshua watched the three men take part of the fence down before cutting a few of the horses out of the herd. Joshua's men had been ordered not to move until he hailed the rustlers.

Joshua waited until they had the horses close to the fence before he stood up and strode forward a few feet. His deputies surrounded the three men on silent feet.

"This is the sheriff speaking. We have you surrounded. Do not attempt to get away or you will be shot. Slowly get off your horses with your hands high in the air."

One of the men swore and tried to pull his gun. Joshua saw it and shot the gun out of the man's hand. The man fell off his horse as he grabbed his hand. Joshua couldn't tell if he had hit the man's hand or the gun. He heard a couple more gunshots and one man grunt in pain.

"You cantankerous ol' outlaw!" Peter exclaimed. "What'd you go and try that for?"

Joshua grinned even as he kept his eye on the man he had shot at—the man he thought to be the leader. He wasn't sure what had happened with the other two, but he knew Micah would fill him in later.

Micah and Joshua handcuffed the men while Daniel and William went to get a wagon. Joshua told the three men to sit down under one of the trees. Micah stood over them with his gun pointed at them.

Joshua turned to the new deputies. "Good job, men. Thank you for your help. I now know who to ask for help if I ever need more deputies."

The three ranch hands smiled. "'Twas our pleasure, Joshua. We didn't want our boss's horses rustled any more than any o' the other ranches."

Joshua laughed. "Point taken, Peter."

Daniel returned with the wagon and the rustlers were loaded up, their horses tied to the back of the wagon.

"I'll drive the wagon, Micah," Joshua said. "You ride alongside us and keep an eye on them."

"Alrighty," Micah replied.

Joshua climbed into the wagon seat and clucked to the horses to get them moving. He was lost in his thoughts for a few minutes before remembering something. "What happened out there anyway, Micah? I kept my attention on the leader the whole time." He gave a sudden laugh. "You know? It's a good thing I trust you guys. I didn't even think that maybe I should keep an eye out on my back. I just trusted that you would watch my back for me."

Micah laughed. "It's a good thing I watched it for you then. Well, after you shot at the leader, one of them tried to wheel his horse around and make a break for the other side of the pasture. He's the one Peter called a 'cantankerous ol' outlaw.'" Joshua chuckled at Micah's imitation of Peter's voice.

"The other guy seemed willing enough to get off his horse. Of course, William had a gun aimed right at his head, so that mighta helped a bit."

"Probably. Well, I'm just glad that we got them. I don't envy Pa trying to fix that fence in the dark."

Micah nodded his head. "Me neither."

The rest of the ride was made in silence. At least from the humans. The night animals could be heard everywhere. Crickets, owls, cicadas, and wolves all made their presence known.

"Whoa!" he called to the horses. The horses stopped in front of the sheriff's office and Joshua set the brake before climbing out of the wagon. He tied the horses to the hitching post and waited for Micah to join him. Micah held a gun at the ready while Joshua ordered the three men out of the wagon and into the jail.

Once the three men were locked in their jail cells, Joshua took his first good look at them. His face was grim when he recognized the two brothers. "Walter and Charles O'Hare, I believe," he said.

Charles nodded. "You must've seen our wanted poster."

Joshua chuckled. "Which one are you referring to? I've seen at least three for you two." He turned to the other man, the one he had not seen on any wanted poster.

"You on the other hand are an anomaly. I have not seen you on a wanted poster. Why is that? Was this your first outlaw activity?"

The red-haired man glared at the sheriff's boots. "No. I've done other things that are so-called outlaw activity. I keep to m'self."

Joshua nodded. "Very smart. But, now that you have been caught, you need to tell me your name."

The red-haired man gritted his teeth and continued to look at the floor, keeping a sullen silence.

Joshua waited almost a full minute for an answer before turning to the O'Hare brothers. "What's his name?" he asked, jerking his thumb toward the red-haired man.

Charles and Walter looked at each other and then at their partner as if trying to figure out their options. They decided to stay silent, so Joshua turned back to the man.

"I can't just keep calling you 'Mister.'" Joshua kept a stern look on his face. "What's your name?"

The man was silent for another minute. "Jed. Jed Stuart," he finally spat.

"Jed?" Joshua asked. "Interesting."

Jed's head snapped up to face Joshua. "What?"

"I met an outlaw a couple years ago whose name was Jed."

Jed finally looked at Joshua's face, and his face and eyes hardened until Joshua wondered if they would be able to break granite.

"You're the kid!" Jed spat. "You're the kid that got away from me with his little sister! Do you have any idea what you put me through?"

Joshua stared at him in confusion. "What do you mean?"

"You killed my partners or helped to kill 'em. You got away from me. Two city kids getting away from one of the best trackers in the woods." His laugh sounded bitter. "You and your sister put me through hell!" He spun on his heel and stalked to the chair in the corner of the cell. Jed straddled the chair, keeping his back to Joshua.

It took Joshua a minute to process Jed's angry outburst. *God, what do You want me to do here? What can I do? Jed needs You. He seems to be angry with Ruth and me. Maybe Ruth was right, maybe he is angry with the world. Help me help him, Lord.*

Joshua glanced at the brothers, who shrugged at him. He smiled. "Jed?"

Jed grunted.

Joshua took a deep breath. "I know you were planning on killing me and Ruth. Those are charges that will not be brought against you. Ruth and I forgave you after we knew we had escaped from you." Joshua waited a few seconds before turning away and walking into his office.

Joshua dropped into his chair, deep in thought.

Micah looked at him with curiosity written all over his face. "What's goin' on in that overworked brain of yours?"

Joshua looked at him distractedly. "Just thinkin'."

"I can see that." He smiled playfully. "What'cha thinking about?"

"Jed Stuart."

His blank stare caused Joshua to laugh a little. "Who?"

"Jed Stuart," Joshua repeated. "He's the red-headed, burly rustler we brought in."

"Why him? I recognized the other two from the wanted posters. But Jed isn't on any of the wanted posters that I can remember."

"I know," Joshua said. "He's a man I saw a couple years ago." Joshua leaned his chin on his hands.

Micah looked at him thoughtfully. "Was he one of the outlaws who robbed the stage you and Ruth came on?"

Joshua nodded. "Yeah. Although, I'm not sure how well we can charge him with it. He recognized me, but he was wearing a mask. Ruth and I can't identify him unless he confesses to the crime."

Micah's eyebrows shot up. "You almost sound like you don't want him to confess."

Joshua stared at the opposite wall. "I'm not sure what I want."

CHAPTER TWENTY ONE

SEPTEMBER 17

*Suspect arrested for stage robbery STOP
Please advise STOP Sheriff Brookings*

SEPTEMBER 17

*Will send lawyer STOP He will take care
of it STOP Wells Fargo*

"Somethin' wrong, Sheriff?" a boy's voice broke into Joshua's reverie.

Joshua looked across his desk at the ten year old blond boy. He smiled, but the smile did not reach his sad eyes. "No, nothing is wrong with me. I'm just disappointed." He stared off into the space behind the boy's head.

Jeremiah looked up at the sheriff with his wide, intelligent brown eyes. "Disappointed about what or by who?"

"Whom," Micah said as he entered the office. "By whom."

"Hiya, Pa!" Jeremiah said.

"Did you hear what I said?" Micah quirked an eyebrow at his son.

Jeremiah ducked his head. "Yes, Sir. I heard."

Joshua watched with an amused look on his face. He loved watching the father and son relationship Jeremiah and Micah had together. It reminded him so much of his own.

"Now repeat your question properly. I, for one, would like to hear the answer." Micah winked at Jeremiah.

Jeremiah turned back to Joshua. "Disappointed about what or by whom?" He emphasized the last word with a mischievous sidelong glance at his pa.

Joshua chuckled at the antics of the deputy and his son. "Just this telegram I received today. The stagecoach company is sending their lawyer out to handle Jed's case."

Micah sat down in one of the chairs. "You've really taken a liking to the outlaw, haven't you?"

Joshua nodded.

"Why?" Jeremiah asked.

Joshua stood up and looked out the window at the street. Turning toward the boy, he answered the question. "I take an interest in all those who are ruining their lives in sin, especially those about to die for their sins. They need to know they will live eternally and that they can only get to heaven through Jesus Christ." He sighed and let his shoulders sag as he leaned against the wall. He kept his voice quiet. "Jed's not ready to die. I had been hoping the company would not press charges since the robbery happened almost two years ago."

"Isn't there some way to work around the charges?" Micah asked.

Joshua grunted. "You know that's not the way I work. The best I have come up with is that Jed was unidentifiable by either Ruth or me. The problem is that if Jed confesses, he will be convicted."

Jeremiah squinted his eyes. "Why do you want him to live?"

Joshua looked at Jeremiah with unseeing eyes. "I'm not sure, exactly," he stated. "Well, obviously, I want him to live until he realizes his sin and repents, but that isn't everything." He kept standing there for a few minutes. At least he thought it was just a few minutes.

When he came back to reality, he saw that Jeremiah and Micah had slipped out of the office. Joshua shrugged. "If anyone can get through to Jed, maybe Ruth can."

He walked out of the office to find Micah. Micah sat on the bench outside and nodded as Joshua stepped through the door.

"I'm heading out to the ranch for a little while." Joshua stopped abruptly. "On second thought, could Jeremiah ride out there and ask Ruth to come here to see me?"

Micah cocked his eyebrow in thought. "Sure. Jeremiah can do that. I'll go tell him." He grinned. "You know how much Jeremiah loves to spend time with Ruth."

"That boy really needs a mother," Joshua retorted.

Micah's grin disappeared. "I know. I just haven't found someone willing to marry a deputy, let alone one with a wild son like Jeremiah."

Joshua smiled. "I suppose it would be rather difficult."

Micah nodded his head. "I'll go get Jeremiah."

Joshua walked back into the office. Just as he was about to sit down behind his desk, he had an idea. He walked to the door leading to the jail.

"Jed?"

Jed sat on the edge of his cot, head in his hands. "What?" he snarled, glaring up at Joshua.

Joshua pulled a chair to the bars and sat on it. "I want to help you, but I can't if you don't let me. I need to know if you want help or not."

Joshua sat silently while Jed continued to glare at him.

"Why would you want to help me? I was supposed to kill you." There was fire in his eyes. "I wanted to kill you and your sister." His voice had a mean edge to it and his laugh was bitter. "I wouldn't mind help, but how do I know what kind of help you'll give me?"

"You will just have to trust me," Joshua replied. He sat deep in thought for a couple of minutes, feeling Jed's eyes boring into him. "I think the best thing for you to do is to write out your story." Joshua stood and looked Jed full in the face.

His face betrayed his shock. "What!?!"

"It would help me know what you have done so I can defend you in court. Either that, or you just tell it to me out loud, right now, right here."

"You? Defend me?" he asked, an incredulous tone in his voice.

"Yes."

Jed stared at him, unbelief written in his eyes. "I can't believe you would do that."

Joshua looked into his skeptical eyes. "Well, start believing. If you tell me your story, I will defend you to the best of my ability."

"Why? What do you get out of it?"

Joshua paused. "Nothing."

"Then why do it?"

How do I explain this, Lord? He is not a believer. For all I know, he has never touched a Bible or heard about You. How do I explain why I want to do this?

Joshua swallowed hard while his mind raced. "Because I believe everyone deserves a chance to get to heaven. Everybody will live eternally after death, some in hell and some in heaven. You are the one who chooses where you will go by choosing or rejecting Jesus' gift to you."

Jed's glare softened somewhat. "I'll write it out," he grunted before turning his back on Joshua.

Joshua had the feeling that Jed still didn't believe him, but was desperate enough to grasp at anything. He smiled. "Thank you. I will go get you some paper and a pencil."

Joshua walked back to his desk and started rummaging through the drawers for a pencil when he heard a female voice above him. He cringed inside. *How did Ruth and Annabelle ever become friends?* he asked himself for the millionth time. *They are such opposites.*

"What are you doing?" Annabelle asked.

"Getting some paper and a pencil out of my desk," Joshua stated. "Can I help you with something, Miss?"

She looked at him with her nose slightly raised. "I just came to see what the great sheriff was doing. What are you going to do with the paper?"

"Our prisoner wants some paper."

"What? You are giving paper to a criminal?" Her voice could be sweet when she wanted it to be, but now was not one of those times.

"He wants to write something."

"And why would a criminal want to write something?" Her voice had a sharp tone to it.

Ever since Annabelle and Ruth had become friends—and then with Annabelle moving to town—she seemed to find time to bother him at least once a week. He tried to keep his voice calm and even. "It really isn't any of your business—"

Annabelle's eyes went wide. "Does he want to write something incriminating?" She laughed. "Oh, silly me. Why would he do that?"

"It is none of your business," Joshua snapped as he finally found the pencil he was looking for. He slapped the pencil on top of the paper and stood.

He sighed heavily as Annabelle stared at him with wide eyes. He had never snapped at her before. "I'm sorry, Annabelle. I shouldn't have snapped at you like that. Please forgive me?"

She looked at him in shock and finally stammered, "Of course. I'll see you later." She turned to leave.

"Ruth will be in town soon. Should I ask her to stop by your house?"

Annabelle's eyes glittered. "Would you? I would love to see Ruth."

"Bye, Annabelle." *Why are women so hard to understand?*

CHAPTER TWENTY TWO

Jed couldn't believe his bad luck. He had been caught for the first time in his outlaw life and the man who had caught him was the kid from the last stage he had robbed. Just when he'd thought his luck had changed.

Jed shook the thoughts out of his mind. He had to stop going down this road. Jed heard a door open and realized that Joshua had left the door to his office open.

Jed's eyebrows shot up when he saw the girl. She looked like a rich, snobby girl who had too much money and time on her hands. If she hadn't been so fancied up, she might even be attractive. In the clothes she had on now, she looked too high and mighty for anyone but a dandy to care about.

Jed looked back as he heard the girl talking to Joshua. His eyes narrowed as he watched the girl's expressive eyes. He grunted. *No doubt 'bout it. She likes him. I wonder if he returns the favor. If it even is a favor.* He strained his ears.

"It's none of your business," Joshua snapped.

No, he smirked, *I don't think he does.* Served the girl right. The girl left the office and Jed swiftly wiped the smirk off his face when he heard Joshua's footsteps.

"Here's the paper and a pencil. Let me know when the pencil gets dull and I will sharpen it for you."

Jed walked to the bars to take the offered items. He nodded his agreement.

Joshua looked like he was about to say something more, but changed his mind. "I'll leave you to your writing." He turned and walked away, closing the door behind him.

Jed stared at the closed door for a couple of minutes before turning to the small desk. He sat down on the hard wooden chair and started his bad attempt at writing his story.

Where to start? That's the thousand dollar question, ain't it? Jed tapped the end of the pencil on the desk. *I'll start when I left Da. That'll be good enough.* He started writing.

Half an hour later, Jed had finished writing about his first real job with the gang. He stood up and stretched his arms over his head. *Why did I choose to write instead of just tell it to that sheriff? Huh.*

Right. Because that sheriff is just a kid who happened to outwit me. One of two kids I was s'pose to kill. He put his hands in the small of his back and stretched backwards. Writing was too hard on the back.

Jed paced the cell. Up eight steps, turn, down eight steps, turn. Back and forth he paced until he heard the door between the cells and the office open again. He sighed, hoping it wouldn't be Joshua, but knowing it probably was.

When the faint smell of flowers reached him, he jerked in surprise. Then again, maybe a visit from Joshua would be preferable to having some female visitor. Jed turned to face the woman.

"Jed?" The voice held a slight tremor in it. Just like it had the day he had robbed the stage. Jed looked up at the young woman.

"Jed?" she asked again.

"Yeah, that's me," Jed snapped.

"I'm Ruth Brookings, Joshua's sister." Ruth pulled a nearby chair closer to her side of the bars and sat on it, facing him. "Joshua just told me you were here."

Jed couldn't help it. He just couldn't stop staring at her. Ruth was so different from that other girl who had come to visit Joshua. Ruth's hair was brown and put up in a simple bun. Her clothes were made of durable cotton and were much more modest and attractive. She was much more grown up since the last time he'd seen her. And he'd been wanting to kill this young woman?

Jed clenched his jaw. He couldn't think that way. "What'd'ya want?" Jed asked.

Ruth looked down at her hands. "I came to tell you that I forgive you. I forgave you even while you were chasing us in the woods." She looked up into his face. Her eyes held no fear. "Are you willing to accept Joshua's help?"

Jed gritted his teeth, eyebrows glowering. "Right now I would accept just about anybody's help. I know there's nothin' he'll be able to do. I don't know why he's wastin' his time with me."

Ruth stood up and took a step closer. "He wants to help you, Jed Stuart. He thinks you can change your ways, even want to change your ways, if you could have a second chance at life."

Jed looked away and shook his head, incredulity written on his face. "Why should I get a second chance? I know what I did was wrong. Everything I did was wrong, but what else was I s'pose to do?" His voice grew hard. "I got a chance to prove m'self and I took it."

Ruth's eyes brimmed with tears. "I don't know what made you think you had to prove yourself, or what made you decide to do what you did, but there is one thing I know for sure. You could have at least stopped doing all those bad things after the stagecoach robbery. You could have decided to change your ways then and lived as a law-abiding citizen."

Jed scoffed at her. "Easy for you to say."

Ruth smiled wryly. "Yes, I suppose it is." She was thoughtful. "God often gives people second chances—"

"Right," Jed interrupted. "Second chances. Where was my mother's second chance at life? If God really cared 'bout me, He wouldn't've had her die givin' birth to me," Jed shouted. "No, I can't believe that God would give me a second chance. I can't believe that anyone, especially God, would do somethin' like that for me."

Jed turned his back on Ruth and stared at the small window sitting in the top of the wall. A few minutes later when he turned around again, she was gone. He'd been so wrapped up in himself that he hadn't heard her leave.

Jed's mind was conflicted. Part of him wanted to believe what Ruth and Joshua had said. But the other part of him knew it wasn't possible. There was no way, no reason, for God to give Jed Stuart a second chance. He didn't deserve it and he knew that without a shadow of a doubt.

CHAPTER TWENTY★THREE

Joshua hadn't intended to overhear Jed and Ruth. The door had been left open and their voices carried. Joshua's heart grew heavy when he heard Jed's words about not believing in second chances. *God,* he prayed, *whatever it takes to bring Jed to You, help me be willing and able to help him. Help me show Your love to him in a way he will understand. Amen.*

After Ruth left, Joshua walked to the doorway of the office and looked out on the main street. The town was quiet. Joshua almost wished something would happen. But, at least he had time to think and pray about what to do for Jed. He knew that Jed would not believe God loved him unless he was somehow shown unconditional love. The problem was that Joshua had no idea how to show it to him.

Two days after he had given the paper and pencil to Jed, Joshua sat at his desk, deep in thought after reading Jed's story. Jed wasn't the most eloquent writer, and the spelling definitely wasn't the greatest, but Joshua had still been unable to put the papers down. *God, how can You show men like Jed's father compassion? I don't understand how You could allow men like him to live and do that to their own sons.* Joshua closed his eyes and took a shaky breath. *God, give me the words to say to Jed.*

The anger Jed felt had been communicated into his written words. Joshua admitted to himself that Ruth had been right. Jed really was angry at the world. *How am I supposed to defend a man like Jed?*

Joshua stood and walked to the jail cell where Jed sat on his cot. "Why, Jed? Why?"

Jed's head jerked up and he glared at Joshua. "Why what?" he growled.

"Why did you always choose the lawless way? Why not choose to live a law-abiding life?"

Jed shrugged.

"You must've had a reason," Joshua persisted.

"Why do I need a reason?"

Joshua drew his eyebrows together in confusion. "Everything is done for a reason."

Jed sighed. "Maybe." They were both quiet. Jed was the first to break the silence. "My first choice after running away from Da was to die or join the outlaw group. After that, it just became my way of

260

life." Jed's voice turned bitter. "Even when I did get an honest job working on a ranch, I ended up doin' killing because I was a known gunfighter."

Joshua stood at the bars, deep in thought. He tried to say something but Jed spoke again, the words nearly spitting out of his mouth.

"Now do you see why I don't deserve a second chance? You read my story. You read all the things I did. I'm rotten to the core. Beyond cure. Beyond hope." His eyes flashed with the fire of hatred and anger. "It's pointless for you to try to help me. I know I'll be sentenced to hang. No one can save me from that."

Joshua looked Jed in the eyes. "God can save you from eternal death. He still loves you, despite your sins." Jed kept his eyes from making contact with Joshua's. "I will still help you in any way I can. I believe that there is still hope. Maybe just a slim chance at it, but it is still there." Joshua spoke with an urgency he rarely used. "You are not rotten to the core. I believe you still have some good hiding down in your heart somewhere. There is still hope for you."

A sudden idea came to him. "I'll be right back."

Joshua rushed to his desk, pulled out one of the New Testaments he kept there, flipped through the pages, and marked two with pieces of paper. His pencil scribbled on each of them. As soon as he was done, he returned to Jed's cell.

"The first passage I marked in this book is about Saul of Tarsus in Acts chapter nine. He was supposedly beyond hope, too, but God gave him a second chance. I encourage you to read it. I think it will help."

Joshua handed it through the bars and Jed took it. He read the title. "The Bible? I should've known." He threw it toward his bed and it bounced off onto the stone floor.

Joshua shook his head, a grin forming on his face. "Yes, it is a Bible. Just try it. You might be surprised how much you like it once you get started."

Joshua saw the glare Jed gave him and left so Jed could think while he prayed.

Micah was in the office when Joshua came through the door.

"Micah?"

"Yep."

"I'm going out. I'll leave you here to watch the office."

"You got it, Sheriff."

Out of habit, Joshua looked up and down the street as he stepped out of the office. Nothing but dust and a few people walking to and from the stores. He turned to his right and strode to the telegraph office.

After sending the telegram to Cheyenne, he walked down to the livery where he stabled his horse, Poseidon, during the day.

"Hey, there, Boy." Joshua brushed his hand down the gelding's flanks. "How would you like to take a ride out to the ranch?" He laughed when Poseidon snorted and moved his head up and down. "Okay, we'll get going. But first I need to get you saddled. I'm not riding bareback."

After saddling his horse, Joshua mounted and directed the horse toward home. As he rode, he studied the scenery and prayed. "God, I know this idea came from You. No one else could have given it to me. Thank You for giving me the idea. I pray that it will work and that she will be willing and able to come out here. God, You know how much Jed needs to accept Your free gift. He is drowning in his anger. Show him Your love."

Joshua rode in silence until he reached the Double B Ranch. He considered visiting his family, but he needed to get back to town. The time would be better spent with God anyway. With his job as sheriff plus helping out at the ranch as needed, Joshua had little time to spend just praying and listening.

Joshua pulled on the reins to direct Poseidon back toward town. Poseidon was reluctant to go away from the ranch, but he was obedient to his master.

"Humans could learn a lot from horses, Poseidon. It takes a lot to break the wildness out of you, but once you are broken, you are forever obedient to your master, as long as they don't mistreat you." He looked around at the rolling hills. "God, help me be completely broken by You and always obey without question."

The rest of the ride was quiet except for the clip-clop of Poseidon's hooves on the packed dirt road. Joshua felt a peace he hadn't felt in some time. He unsaddled his horse and let him loose in the corral at the livery. He didn't have all the answers yet to his questions about how to help Jed, but he knew they would come if he waited patiently for them.

Joshua whistled his favorite hymn as he strode back to the sheriff's office. Soon this matter would all be cleared up and work out for God's glory.

CHAPTER TWENTY FOUR

Jed heard Joshua talking to the deputy and felt strangely disappointed when he heard the door close. He stared at the closed wooden door that separated the jail cells from the sheriff's office.

"What'cha lookin' at?" a voice broke into his thoughts.

Jed shook his head and looked around to see the man who had spoken. He saw a man sitting in the cell that Charles and Walter had been in until a couple days before. The O'Hare brothers had been moved to Cheyenne. The man in the other cell was an obvious drunk. His hair and clothes were filthy, he had a protruding beer belly, and the smell that came from him was overpowering even from a distance.

"Nothin'," Jed replied.

The drunk stood up and stretched. "What's the book the sheriff gave ya?"

"Nothin'."

"Not very talkative, are ya?" The man shook his head and walked back to his cot. Jed watched in silence as the man collapsed onto the cot before swinging his legs up and lying down with a groan. *The man is a mess. Doesn't he know what he's doin' to himself?*

Jed turned his back on the man and stumbled to the only surface he could sit on besides the hard-as-rock straight back chair. His foot hit something as he reached the bed. He glanced down and muttered a curse under his breath. He clenched his jaw and sank onto the cot. The cot sagged and creaked under his weight.

Why did Joshua have to give me a Bible? Didn't he know that God was the last person anywhere to be interested in Jed Stuart? If God had been int'rested in me, He would've done somethin' about my life a long time ago. But no! Jed thought bitterly. *God did nothin'. He never stopped me from doin' anything. He never did anythin' for me.*

Except give you life, a voice from his past said.

Jed's head fell and he closed his eyes, trying to block out the flood of memories. Anna. His sister had tried her hardest to soothe Jed after his da's beatings. She had raised him, though just a child herself. Jed scowled. *I'm not so sure it wouldn't have been better not to live. If I'd died and Ma'd lived, everybody would've been happier.*

Jed glanced at the form of the man in the other cell. He was asleep. For a split second, Jed wondered how long the man would be in the cell. Probably not long.

Looking around his cell again he tried to find something to occupy his time. He was not used to sitting still in a cramped living area. He was a man of the woods, used to wide spaces and the outdoors.

Stone wall, more stone wall, small window too high up to see out of, another stone wall, metal bars set into a stone wall frame.

Lowering his gaze, he looked at the small writing desk. He wondered if it was supposed to be a table. The paper and pencil still sat on the desktop. He had already done more writing than he had ever intended to do. The chair sat at the desk looking as uncomfortable as it was to sit on.

The floor was made of stone and hid things, especially dirt, very well. It just about hid the Bible that Jed thought he'd kicked under the cot. The Bible hid well enough that Jed almost didn't see it. But he did. His hand started to reach for it. He jerked his arm back with a force that all but knocked him backwards. He would not read that book!

Jed stood up and angrily paced the eight steps across the room. Back and forth, back and forth. Hands clasped behind his back. Hands hanging at his sides. Hands in front of him. Hands on his head pulling his hair out. He was going to go crazy in here!

He started pacing from the back to the front. Only six steps that way because of the cot. Back and forth. Back and forth. His foot caught on something and he let out a string of curses as his knees hit the hard stone floor. His right hand brushed the object. Another curse left his mouth as he realized what had tripped him: the Bible. Unbidden, a saying from his past spoke to him: "God's Word is a stumbling block to those who do not believe."

Jed snarled and tossed the book toward the bars. His face pulled upward into an evil grin when he saw the Bible sail through the bars of his cell and land just outside the bars where the drunk was. *Serves You right, God,* he thought with satisfaction.

Jed allowed himself to take deep breaths for the first time in hours. He lay down on his back. The cot was uncomfortable, but he was feeling a bit tired. He closed his eyes and was almost relaxed when he heard a voice.

"This the book the sheriff gave you?"

Jed grimaced. The nasally voice of the drunk grated on his nerves. He chose to ignore the man, hoping that he would take the hint.

Jed heard the book slide across the floor and assumed that the drunk was somehow trying to fish it through the bars of his cell.

"Y'know, my ma used to read to me from the Bible. I never thought I'd miss it, but she might've been right about one thing. You know what that was?"

The drunk waited a few seconds and Jed guessed he was waiting for Jed's answer. Jed refused to give him the pleasure.

"'Course you don't. Anyway, she always claimed this Bible reading would help keep me on the 'straight and narrow,' as she called it. If I woulda listened to her, I probably would've."

Jed heard pages rustling.

"Huh. Sheriff must've marked a passage for you to read. You read it yet?"

Another couple seconds of silence.

"Not much of a talker, are ya?" the drunk asked. He gave a quiet chuckle. "Let's see here..."

Jed heard the drunk's cot creak as he sat down.

"Ahh. Acts chapter nine. 'And Saul, yet breathing out threatenings and slaughter against the disciples of the Lord...' Now those are some mighty powerful words, don'tcha think?"

Jed's eyes had opened as the drunk read the words and he stared at the man in the other cell. *This is in the Bible? I thought all Bible stories were about perfect people. This man was undeniably not a Christian or even a Bible believer, was he?*

Jed tried to feign indifference, but the drunk looked at him and gave him a look that seemed to mean that he knew exactly what Jed was thinking.

"I think I'll continue. This story gets mighty interestin'. 'And he was three days without sight, and neither did eat nor drink.' Phewee! That be a long time to go without food or water."

Jed saw the drunk shake his head.

"'And there was a certain disciple at Damascus, named Ananias; and to him said the Lord in a vision, "Ananias." And he said, "Behold, I am here, Lord." And the Lord said unto him, "Arise, and go into the street which is called Straight, and enquire in the house of Judas for one called Saul, of Tarsus: for, behold, he prayeth, And hath seen in a vision a man named Ananias coming in, and putting his hand on him, that he might receive his sight.'" Can you imagine bein' this Ananias fellow?" the drunk interjected. "He's gotta be one o' them Christian fellows Saul was akillin' and now the Lord is tellin' him to go to Saul and heal 'im? I know I sure wouldn'ta done it."

Jed grunted and regretted it as soon as he'd done so.

"I knew you was listenin'," the drunk cackled. "Well, since you seem so int'rested in the story, I'll continue. 'Then Ananias answered, "Lord, I have heard by many of this man, how much evil he hath done to thy saints at Jerusalem: And here he hath authority from the chief priests to bind all that call on thy name.'" Smart man," the drunk said. "Very smart man."

Jed saw him blink his eyes a few times.

"Now where was I? Oh, yes. 'But the Lord said unto him, "Go thy way: for he is a chosen vessel unto me, to bear my name before the Gentiles, and kings, and the children of Israel: For I will shew him how great things he must suffer for my name's sake." And Ananias went his way, and entered into the house; and putting his hands on him said, "Brother Saul, the Lord, even Jesus, that appeared unto thee in the way as thou camest, hath sent me, that thou mightest receive thy sight, and be filled with the Holy Ghost."'"

Jed watched the drunk raise an eyebrow at him and give a half grin.

"Now wasn't that nice of ol' Ananias?" the drunk asked.

Jed glared at him and the drunk had the decency to look uncomfortable and clear his throat a few times.

"'And immediately there fell from his eyes as it had been scales: and he received sight forthwith, and arose, and was baptized.' Now that's quite int'restin'. Any idea what this baptism stuff is?"

Jed ignored the question; he was already lost in his own thoughts. *That was awfully quick, wasn't it, Saul? Just like that... Well,* he admitted to himself reluctantly, *I s'pose that if God had come to me in a vision that blinded me, I might've made it that quick, too.*

"What's this?" he heard the drunk mutter. "Hmm, methinks it's a note fer you." The drunk walked to the bars of his cell and tossed the Bible in Jed's direction.

Jed walked to the bars and picked up the Bible. He opened it up to the bookmark and read the note. "'Open up to the next bookmark and read verses 11-17 of chapter one.'"

Jed sat there for a minute just holding the Bible open in his lap, staring at the pages. Curiosity got the better of him and he opened the Bible to the next bookmark. "Chapter one verses eleven through seventeen," he muttered.

"'But I certify you, brethren, that the gospel which was preached of me is not after man. For I neither received it of man, neither was I taught it, but by the revelation of Jesus Christ. For ye have heard of my conversation in time past in the Jews' religion, how that beyond measure I persecuted the church of God, and wasted it: And profited in the Jews' religion above many my equals in mine own nation, being more exceedingly zealous of the traditions of my fathers.

"'But when it pleased God, who separated me from my mother's womb, and called me by his grace, To reveal his Son in me, that I might preach him among the heathen; immediately I conferred not with flesh and blood: Neither went I up to Jerusalem to them which were apostles before me; but I went into Arabia, and returned again unto Damascus.'"

Jed closed the Bible, put it on the desk, and stretched out on the cot, arms under his head. He stared at the stone and mortar ceiling and thought about what he had just read. His thoughts leaned in God's favor for the first time in over ten years.

CHAPTER TWENTY FIVE

Joshua looked up from the wanted posters. He smiled when he saw a very eager young boy standing by his desk.

"What is it, Jeremiah?"

"Telegram for you, Sheriff," Jeremiah said with a grin that matched Joshua's.

Joshua took the telegram. "Thank you, Jeremiah. Wait here while I read it. I might want you to take a reply back."

Jeremiah nodded.

Joshua skimmed the telegram. He closed his eyes and breathed a sigh of relief. *Thank You, Lord!* Elizabeth would be coming, as would her father. "How good is your memory, Jeremiah?"

Jeremiah furrowed his eyebrows and jerked back slightly. "I think it's pretty good. Why?"

"Can you remember a message that I tell you?"

Jeremiah gave a half smile. "Depends on how long it is."

Joshua smiled. "It isn't very long."

"Try me."

"Okay, here it is. 'Elizabeth and Edward STOP Come soon STOP Time is running out STOP Lodging will be provided STOP Sheriff Brookings.' Got it, Jeremiah?"

Jeremiah repeated it back to Joshua word perfect. Joshua nodded with a satisfied smile on his face. "Good! Jeremiah?"

"Yeah?"

Joshua's smile disappeared. "What was said in the telegram shouldn't be repeated anywhere."

"Okay." Jeremiah shrugged. "Who're Elizabeth and Edward?"

Joshua shook his head. "I can't say. Now go tell it to the telegraph man and get it sent."

"Yes, Sir!" Jeremiah ran as fast as he could out of the office and down the street.

Joshua shook his head, laughing. "Oh, to have that much energy again."

Two days later, a young woman and older man stepped from the stagecoach. Joshua moved forward to greet them. He held out his hand to the gentleman. The man wore a brown broadcloth suit and Joshua could tell he was jovial from the laugh lines on his tanned face. "I am Sheriff Brookings. You are the Harrises?"

Edward Harris looked him up and down. "Yes, we are. You are much younger than I expected."

Miss Harris laughed and Joshua turned toward her. "I am sorry. I usually don't laugh so rudely."

Joshua grinned at the brown-haired young lady. His quick eyes took in her tasteful, simple, and attractive dark-green dress. The dress set off the deep green in her eyes and he couldn't help but notice the mischievous twinkle in her eyes. "Not a problem, Miss Harris. I was about to laugh myself, but you beat me to it." Turning back to Mr. Harris, he responded, "I have heard that before. I became sheriff out of necessity and was voted in a month later." He shrugged. "I guess the townspeople think I do a decent enough job."

Mr. Harris's gaze softened into a smile. "Yes, they must. I suppose I shouldn't be too surprised. I had heard something about there being a young sheriff up this way who had been doing a splendid job." He looked around at the buildings. "Where are we to stay?"

"My father and mother insisted that you stay at their ranch. I have a sister who is dying to meet you, Miss Harris," Joshua said with a smile.

"Please just call me Elizabeth," Elizabeth said with a wave of her hand. "I would love to meet your sister. And stay on a ranch. What kind of ranch is it?"

Joshua picked up one of the trunks and started walking toward the wagon he had borrowed. "Pa has a horse ranch. We raise, breed, and sell the best horses in the West."

"Really?" Mr. Harris said with skepticism.

Joshua laughed. "Well, maybe not quite that good, but the Army seems to like them better than any other horses being sold in the Montana and Wyoming Territories."

Joshua and Mr. Harris loaded the two trunks into the wagon bed. As he prepared the horses, he turned to Elizabeth. *Was it too early to ask the question burning in his mind?* "Would you prefer to see Jed today or tomorrow, Elizabeth?"

Elizabeth swallowed hard and gave a shaky smile. "Tomorrow. I don't think I'm quite ready to see him yet."

Joshua nodded and helped Elizabeth up onto the wagon seat. Mr. Harris climbed in on the other side. Once they were all situated, Joshua clucked to the horses and they started their bumpy ride to the Double B Ranch.

Joshua pointed out some of the most attractive landmarks along the road to the ranch. After listening to the old-timers talk about the area for the last couple of years, he had stories about each landmark to tell. Elizabeth and her father laughed many times during the short trip.

"And here is the entrance to the ranch. There's an interesting story there, too. Apparently, this land used to belong to a rich man. The problem was that he hoarded all his money, didn't even trust the bank with it. He buried it all on his land and lived like a pauper. Died like one, too. No one knew where he hid his money and there were a lot of fortune seekers who dug up this land.

"One of the old-timers thinks that's why the dirt is so rich here. Because it was dug up so much, it got more air and loosened up the dirt instead of being beaten down or washed away in the rains. None of the money was found and people decided that the rich man had lied about having any money.

"While we were digging the fence posts for the fence here, William hit something real hard just a few feet down. His ankle hurt for a couple days because he jarred it so bad. When we got it dug out, we found a small treasure chest full of gold. After hearing the story about the rich guy, we tracked down his heir and gave it to her. And although she was quite poor, she gave us a third of the gold since we had found it there."

"That was so sweet of her," Elizabeth exclaimed. "I can't believe the fortune hunters didn't find it."

Joshua shrugged. "Me neither. My only guess is they didn't think he would've hid it so close to the road."

Joshua glanced at Elizabeth and saw her looking at the landscape.

"I wish I could've been here when this was built. It is so lovely here!" Elizabeth cried.

"Wait until you see the view from the house," Joshua said with a grin. "You will fall in love with it immediately. If you don't, you obviously have something wrong with you."

Mr. Harris chuckled. "Is it that good?" he asked.

Joshua nodded. "It is."

Poseidon carried Joshua back into Cartersville after he had spent an hour getting the Harrises settled with his family. His smile was still attached from ear to ear when he walked into his office.

"What's that grin for?" Micah asked.

"The Harrises are great people," Joshua replied. "They fit into the family quite well. Even though they are guests and just met us, they acted like they had known us for ages." Joshua laughed as he remembered something that had happened. "I could tell Pa liked Elizabeth. He started teasing her nearly from the moment he saw her. And the best part? She teased him right back."

Micah chuckled. "So your pa finally found his match in teasing?"

Joshua grinned. "I think he did."

Micah shook his head. "It took long enough."

"I know. You would think that with five kids, one of them would have had some comebacks for him or at least be able to give as good as they received. But, no, it takes a complete stranger from Wyoming to finally set Pa in his place." Joshua chuckled. "I can hardly believe it. Especially with everything she has been through."

Micah's smile faded and confusion settled on his face. "What do you mean?"

Joshua shook his head and frowned. "Never mind. I shouldn't have said that. I'm not supposed to tell anyone. This is between Jed and Elizabeth and now me."

Micah nodded. "I'll just forget that you ever said anything about it." He stood and stretched. "When is Elizabeth coming?"

"Tomorrow morning. Can you do the morning patrol of the town?"

Micah nodded. "Sure. I can do that."

"Thanks. I just feel like I should be here when Elizabeth and Jed meet. Pray for them, especially Jed. He doesn't know she is here and I'm not sure how he will react. It's going to be hard on Elizabeth, too."

"I'll pray for them."

"Can I pray, too, Pa?" a young voice broke into the conversation.

Micah looked down. "How'd you sneak in here?"

"I'm practicin' my Indian walking," Jeremiah said proudly. "It worked, too. I walked so quiet, you never even heard me. Can I pray, too?"

Micah laughed and shook his head. "Yes, you can pray about anything, Jeremiah."

"Jed's the man in jail, right?" Jeremiah asked.

Joshua nodded. "Yes."

"I've already been praying that he will find Jesus."

"Thank you, Jeremiah. I'm sure he will appreciate the prayers once he accepts Jesus' gift to him," Joshua said. "I just hope it is soon. The trial is next week."

Jeremiah stared at the door to the jail. "He will. I know he will do it before the end of the trial."

"The faith of a child," Joshua said quietly. "I wish I had faith like that."

Jeremiah shrugged. "What's he charged with?"

"Rustling, horse stealing, murder, and robbery."

"Jeremiah," Micah interrupted, "does Mrs. Tucker know where you are?"

"No, not exactly, but I'm sure she could find me if she needed to."

"What if she needs you and doesn't have time to go looking for you? You know she's the fourth we've had in the last two years. If you keep disappearing like this, she'll probably leave, too," Micah said, eyebrows raised.

"I'm on my way home, Pa," Jeremiah said cheerfully. "Thanks for the reminder. I'll be prayin'." With that, Jeremiah raced out the door.

"Does that boy ever run out of energy?" Joshua asked.

Micah grunted. "I've never seen him run out of it. He even moves the whole time he is sleeping."

Joshua raised his eyebrows. "Really?"

Micah laughed. "Really. He tosses and turns the whole night long. Ever since he was a baby. Edith swore something was wrong with him, but the doc never could find anything wrong. He's always been a restless, wanderin' boy."

"Maybe he'll be the next Christopher Columbus," Joshua said.

"Maybe."

Joshua looked up at the clock and sighed. "Well, it's time for taking a turn around the town. I'll go this time."

Micah nodded. "Don't find any trouble. I kind of like living in a quiet town."

"I only find trouble when there actually is some."

"Uh-huh," Micah said, unconvinced.

"What is that supposed to mean?"

Micah laughed. "Nothin'. Now, go make the rounds. Somebody might need to be caught makin' trouble."

"I thought I was the one in charge," Joshua retorted.

"You are, but you are moving awfully slow today, so I thought you might need a bit of a push."

"Okay, okay. I'm going. See you later, Deputy."

CHAPTER TWENTY SIX

Elizabeth rose early the next morning. She loved being on a ranch again. It had been years since she had stayed at her cousin's ranch. The fresh air, the slight smell of manure and fresh-cut hay were a thrill to her nose.

After dressing hurriedly into her light-green calico dress, she walked softly down to the kitchen in the semi-dark. It wasn't quite dawn yet and she went out onto the porch to watch the sunrise. Elizabeth paused in the doorway when she saw the shadow of a person already standing on the porch. The man turned.

"Come on out, Elizabeth." Daniel Brookings beckoned to her. "I see you are also an early riser."

Elizabeth smiled. "Yes, I am. I love to see the sunrise in the mornings. It is so peaceful and beautiful." She looked around. The mountains behind the house were just a shadow in the darkness. "I can't imagine how lovely the sunset must be against those mountains." Her laugh was low and quiet. "But, I suppose I will have to wait until tonight to find out."

Daniel laughed with her. "Yes, I suppose you will."

Elizabeth sat on the porch swing to wait for the sunrise. Both of them waited in mutual silence as the minutes ticked past. Elizabeth wondered what it must be like to live out here among the rolling hills of Montana. She took deep breaths and let out a contented sigh.

Thank You, Lord, for bringing me out here to this beautiful ranch. May I find a way to be a blessing to this kind family to repay them for their hospitality to Father and me. And Lord, give me the words to say to Jed when I talk to him later today. Calm my heart and my nerves. Give me a willing and forgiving spirit. Open Jed's heart to the words You have for me to say to him. Thank You for all You do for me every day. Bless the Brookings family and lead them forever on the path You have chosen.

The wispy clouds began to show a warm gold and pink pattern and Elizabeth knew the sun's disk would soon be peeking above the shadowy hills. The sky continued to brighten. Elizabeth watched, enraptured at the sight. Never had she seen a sunrise like this, the rich purples, golds, pinks, yellows, and reds all blending and intermingling together. The thin, wispy clouds scattering and skittering across the sky as the sun began its slow ascent over the distant hills.

Unconscious of her own movement, Elizabeth soon found herself standing next to Daniel. They gave each other a brief smile before turning their attention back to God's ever-changing painting.

"I wish I were a painter," Elizabeth whispered. "This sunrise is too beautiful not to be enjoyed by others."

"I always say that those who rise early to enjoy the sunrise are the most blessed because of it," Daniel replied. "They get to see a beauty few others do."

Elizabeth nodded her head in a gentle movement. "Yes. Yes, they do."

Time slipped by unnoticed as Elizabeth watched the sun become fully visible above the hill. The vibrant colors faded away as the light grew brighter. Elizabeth tore her eyes from the mesmerizing sight and, with reluctant step, turned back toward the door to the kitchen. She took one last glance at the eastern horizon as she opened the door to help Ruth and Harriet with breakfast. She closed her eyes and took a deep breath before stepping into the kitchen, closing the door behind her.

"When are you going to town, Elizabeth?" Edward Harris asked his daughter as they finished eating breakfast.

"Ruth and I were planning on leaving as soon as breakfast was cleaned up," Elizabeth replied.

"If that is all right, Father?" Ruth asked. "I thought I could go visit with Annabelle while Elizabeth talked to Jed."

Daniel nodded. "That sounds like a wonderful plan, Ruth. You can give Elizabeth moral support as well as making sure she makes it to town."

Ruth and Elizabeth scurried around the kitchen cleaning off the table, washing and drying the dishes, and getting ready for their visit to town.

"I'm ready," Ruth announced.

"That makes one of us," Elizabeth said with a nervous laugh.

Ruth patted her on the arm and gave her a reassuring hug. "Let's go. The sooner we leave, the sooner we get there. And the sooner we get there..."

"...The sooner this whole thing is over and done with," Elizabeth laughed. "Thank you, Ruth. I needed that."

Ruth and Elizabeth were both lost in their own thoughts on the drive to town. Ruth drove the buggy while Elizabeth prayed silently for strength. When they arrived in town, Ruth steered the buggy to the livery stable and the owner came out of the barn.

"Joshua said you two might be comin' inta town today."

"Yes, Mr. Pervis, we are here," Ruth said with a smile.

Mr. Pervis grabbed the horses' leads and shooed the two away. "Go on to yer business 'round town. I'll take care o' yer horses."

Elizabeth stepped down from the buggy. "Thank you, Mr. Pervis."

"Don't mention it," the man answered as he led the horses and buggy away.

"You must come here often."

"Yes, I do," Ruth said. "Sometimes in the buggy and sometimes on horseback." They walked down the sidewalk past a few stores. "This is where we part ways." Ruth pointed up the street. "The sheriff's office is four buildings down on the left. It's hard to miss. I'll be over there," she pointed across the street, "in that yellow house with the fancy white trim."

Elizabeth's eyebrows shot up. "Annabelle's house?"

Ruth's half grin told Elizabeth more than any words could have. "Yes," Ruth replied. "Her father made a good living off the ranch and ended up running for mayor, so they moved to town. We are very different, but we somehow became friends anyway." She gave Elizabeth a quick hug. "I will either meet you at the sheriff's office or at Annabelle's house."

"Sounds like a plan." Elizabeth watched Ruth cross the street before turning to walk down to the sheriff's office.

"God, You know I cannot do this without Your help. Please give me the words to say."

Taking a deep breath, Elizabeth paused before opening the heavy wooden door. "Good morning, Sheriff Brookings," she said with a bright smile.

"Elizabeth!" Joshua stood and took off his hat. "It is a pleasure to see you again. Although, I must insist that you use my given name if I am to use yours." He smiled and winked at her. "Please have a seat." Elizabeth began to protest, but Joshua raised his hand for silence. "There are a few things I need to tell you before I let you go in there." He pointed at the door behind him.

Elizabeth sat down and watched Joshua lean against the edge of his desk, arms crossed.

"Elizabeth, Jed Stuart is a very angry man. His anger defines who he is. He thinks he is angry at me and Ruth for getting away from him and making him look like a fool." Joshua paused and looked Elizabeth right in the eyes. "What he doesn't know is that his anger is truly directed at God. God is the One who is making him look like a fool in order to draw him close."

Joshua looked away and moved behind his desk. He collapsed into the chair, staring at the ceiling behind her. "Jed refuses to listen to either Ruth or me because he cannot forgive himself for wanting to kill us. He rejects our offers of help, although he did concede a little by telling me his whole story."

"Why do you think I will be able to help?" Elizabeth asked.

Joshua leaned forward, resting his elbows on his knees. "Because God told me you would. Elizabeth, you are the only person Jed mentioned by name to me. I believe that you are the only person who can truly show him forgiveness and unconditional love." Joshua shut his eyes. "I know it will be hard, but I believe that God had you there in Cheyenne for a reason and now He has you here for a reason." He opened his eyes and turned them to Elizabeth. "God can work through you to help Jed," he finished in a low voice.

Elizabeth sat still, watching her fingers do nothing. She could feel Joshua's eyes on her as she thought. "I know He can," she said in a voice just above a whisper. "Ever since you first contacted me a week ago, I have been praying that He will give me a forgiving and loving spirit as well as the words to say." She took a deep breath and lifted her grief-stricken eyes to meet Joshua's. "I think I'm ready now."

Joshua nodded, stood up, and walked to the door separating the cells and the office. Just as he reached for the doorknob, Elizabeth placed a hand on his shoulder. Joshua turned his head to look at her, a question in his eyes.

"Pray for me while I am in there, please?" she asked.

"I already am," Joshua replied as he turned the knob and opened the door. "He is in the cell straight down the hall. There is a chair outside the cell if you want to sit down."

Elizabeth closed her eyes for a few seconds and took a deep breath. "Thank you, Joshua."

"I'll be right here at my desk praying for you and Jed."

Elizabeth gave him a sad smile and started walking toward Jed. As she neared the cell, she saw Jed's back turned toward her. Her breath caught in her throat. *God, help me!* she pleaded. *I can't do this on my own.*

Swallowing hard, she got as close to the bars as she could before she spoke. She squared her shoulders, tears brimming in her eyes, a sad smile playing with her lips. Her voice cracked when she finally spoke. "Hello, Jed."

CHAPTER TWENTY SEVEN

When the voice spoke behind him, Jed's body jerked. He had heard someone come into the cell area and had assumed that Joshua had come in again to talk to him about God. He'd decided to feign disinterest. He was tired of all the religious talk. It did him no good at all since he was a dead man as soon as the judge arrived.

But that voice. He tried to place it. He stared at the mortar between the stones while he searched his mind in vain. It sounded familiar. *But I don't know that many females. I should be able to figure out which one might be talking to me.*

It wasn't Ruth and it certainly wasn't the girl who was infatuated with Joshua. She would never talk to him. There was no way it would be the girl from Cheyenne...was there?

Jed's curiosity finally got the better of him and he turned around. The young woman who had spoken stood at the bars. *If I reached out, I could touch her...* Jed shook his head and closed his eyes, willing the vision, the ghost from his past, to just leave. *Please leave. I can't talk to you. I can't face my guilt.*

"Jed?" The woman's voice sounded concerned. *What would she be concerned about?*

Jed snapped his eyes open and growled, "What do you want?"

The young woman looked deep into his eyes until he could bear it no longer and looked away.

"Do you even know my name? I don't remember—"

Jed stared at the floor. "Elizabeth Harris." His voice was just above a whisper. "I forced ya to tell it to me. It's a name that haunts my very soul." Jed scuffed the toe of his boot on the floor.

When she responded her words were drawn out. "Yes, I suppose it would." Jed heard a chair scrape against the stones. He was tempted to look up, but refused. There was no way he could look at that girl...woman again.

"Jed, I came here after Joshua told me you had been caught rustling. He wrote to my father and me after he read your story. I wanted to come here to tell you why we never pressed charges against you. I could have described you perfectly. I even knew your name." Her voice stumbled and she gave a shaky laugh.

Her next words betrayed how scattered her thoughts were. "I had never known hate before, not

294

that bad anyway. But that night and the next few days, I was consumed with hatred. I hated you for what you did. I hated everything about you. If I could have gotten out of bed or at least stopped hating you long enough, I probably would have gone to the sheriff and given him anything I happened to know about you."

She paused and Jed heard her take a deep breath. Her next words were so soft, he barely heard them. "I even hated myself. I hated myself for being so stupid. I hated myself for disobeying my father. If I had listened to him, I would not have been out there that night. And Father would not have been forced to somehow keep me from killing myself. I tried twice."

Jed's head snapped up, eyes wide, his breath rasping through his lungs. "Why?" he choked. "Why would you do that?"

Elizabeth smiled through her tears. "Do you know what small towns are like? Even Cheyenne, Wyoming, is considered small. Everybody knows everybody and what goes on with everybody else. It only took two days for the news to spread even though Father tried to keep it quiet.

"When I heard the news had been spread around, I knew I would be shunned by all my friends and society in general because of what you did. I hated you for what you did and I hated myself for letting you get away with it. I hated myself for not listening to Father. I hated myself for turning away from God. And most of all I hated that my dream of ever getting married was now practically nonexistent." Tears were streaming down her face and her voice was quiet, though steady.

Jed strode to the bars, anger at himself and Elizabeth bursting through him. "You had nothin' to do with it! I wouldn't've let you get away or stop me. You know I'm much stronger than you are." Elizabeth nodded. "Why would you hate yourself for what *I* did? It doesn't make any sense! And why make my crime worse by killing yourself?" He fumed to himself, pacing furiously around the small cell. *Why'd I have to get so drunk that night that I couldn't think straight?*

"Women can be rather irrational at times, especially when they are depressed and hurt."

Jed looked over at Elizabeth and saw the slight twinkle in her eyes. He shook his head and turned away. "So ya came all the way from Cheyenne just t' tell me that?"

"No," Elizabeth answered.

"Let me guess," Jed said to the wall, venom lacing his every word. "You came here to tell me that I need God ta live the last of the few days I've left here on earth." He spun around to face her, all of his Irish and Scottish anger burning hot. "Let me tell you something," he said in a low, menacing voice. "I don't need God and God certainly don't want, or need, me. You of all people should know that God'd never accept me."

Elizabeth looked down at the hands in her lap. Jed watched her, anger and hate still in his eyes.

When Elizabeth looked up at him, tears glistened in her eyes again. The chair slid back as she stood and stepped in front of him. "Jed, I forgave you as soon as I truly accepted God's forgiveness of what I had done. Ephesians 4:31-32 says, 'Let all bitterness, and wrath, and anger, and clamour, and evil speaking, be put away from you, with all malice: And be ye kind one to another, tenderhearted, forgiving one another, even as God for Christ's sake hath forgiven you.' Forgiving you was the only way I could have peace with God and the only way God would forgive me.

"I accepted you as the hurting young man you are. I had rebelled against my father, turned my back on God, started spending time with the wrong crowd. I may have never done anything like murder a person, but I still did plenty of wrong things, Jed.

"It wasn't until after you came and tried to ruin my life that God helped me turn my life around. After my two suicide attempts, Father had a talk with me and I finally accepted God as my personal Savior. Oh, I'd said the prayer before, but this time I truly meant it. Jed Stuart, if I—a miserable sinner like yourself, and one who was hurt by you—can accept you, how could God not accept you?"

Jed's breath was shallow as he struggled to control his feelings and the conversation. "Because God is perfect and you aren't," he spat. "If you were perfect—"

"God is perfectly loving, perfectly good, perfectly kind, and perfectly forgiving." Elizabeth put her hands around the bars where Jed had placed his. Their hands were nearly touching. "God forgave you when Jesus died on the cross. He forgave you knowing what you would do after you were born. He forgave you the day you were born. He forgave you the night you—"

Her voice broke and her knuckles turned white as she gripped the bars. She looked straight into Jed's eyes, raw emotion visible even to the densest person. "God forgave you when you stole all those cattle and horses." Her voice dropped to a whisper. "God forgives you even now, Jed. He forgives your unbelief, your sins. Why can't you accept that He would do that?"

Jed's teeth ground together and his jaw began to hurt. He jerked away from the bars and turned his back on Elizabeth. "Go away!" His voice was tense with barely controlled anger. "Just go away!"

Minutes—or was it hours?—later when Jed turned around, Elizabeth was gone. Jed thought her absence would be a relief, but it did nothing to relieve the tension or the anger.

Jed spent the rest of the day feeling miserable and depressed. He tried pacing, but each time he passed the bars or saw the chair, Elizabeth's words came back to him. He tried to sleep. As soon as his eyes closed, Elizabeth's face would be there, filled with compassion, a sweet smile on her face. He tried to read the Bible Joshua had given him, but it held no interest to him.

Finally, he resorted to sitting on the hard wooden chair facing the corner of the cell. He refused to let his brain think about anything at all. When Joshua put the food on his desk, Jed did not turn around and refused to touch the food.

As darkness pervaded the cell, Jed's brain began to calm down and stop thinking about Elizabeth. He lay down on the cot and fell instantly into a dreamless sleep.

The next morning, Jed woke up to the smell of coffee and bacon. He looked at the desk and saw the tray of food. *Did I really sleep that long?* He looked out the window. *I must've.* Shrugging, he sat up, grabbed the tray, and dug into the food.

When the food was gone, his eye caught sight of the chair outside his cell. The chair Elizabeth had sat in yesterday. Somehow, overnight, the anger seemed to have simmered down a little. Jed blinked his eyes in surprise at the thoughts coming to him. *Maybe she was right. Would God really and truly forgive me?* He shook his head in disbelief. *No, He wouldn't. If I were God, I wouldn't want myself in heaven.*

Jed picked the Bible up off the desk and began to flip through it. He had just finished reading a short Psalm when he heard light footsteps approaching his cell. He looked up at the sound. Elizabeth.

Jed groaned when he saw her. *What is she doing here again? Didn't she get enough of me yesterday?* He watched as she walked straight for the bars in front of him.

"Hello, Jed." Her smile was broad and inviting. "I hope you don't mind, but after praying last night, I felt God telling me that I should come here again to make one last appeal to you."

"Appeal?" Jed asked in confusion.

"Yes." Concern pooled in Elizabeth's face. "Jed, we both know that even just the rustling could get you hanged. Even if there isn't enough evidence for the stagecoach robberies, you will most likely be hanged. Soon. Before that happens, you need to make your peace with God. If you don't—"

"I know," Jed interrupted. "I'll go to hell. Maybe I want to."

Elizabeth was taken aback. "Why? Why would you want to go there?"

Jed shrugged. "All my friends'll be there."

"Maybe. But you won't be having a good time and you probably won't even be able to see them. And you will live forever, burning without any relief. If you die without Jesus, you will no longer be in God's merciful presence. Even when you do not follow God's laws here on earth, you are always in God's presence. There is no more miserable life than living without God's mercy. Even living here in this tiny cell with little or nothing to do won't be as bad."

Jed stared at his hands. He heard a light whispering and glanced over at Elizabeth. Her mouth moved and her eyes were closed. His thoughts scattered. *What's she praying about? What if she's right? What if...*

His thoughts were interrupted by a quiet, but strong voice. "Heavenly Father, I come before You with a heavy heart. You know Jed Stuart and that he desperately needs You. Draw him close to You. Help him understand that he needs You and that You truly will accept him for who he is and who he can be, not who he was in the past. Thank You, Father. In Jesus' holy name I pray, amen."

Jed looked across the small cell to where Elizabeth stood. His thoughts were gone; his mind seemed empty. He felt almost at peace while Elizabeth prayed for him.

"I will leave you alone now. Read John chapter three if you feel like reading something." Elizabeth smiled and turned, walking with confidence down the hallway and out the door.

Jed had the sudden feeling of having lost his best friend. *Will I ever see her again?*

A small voice in his head replied, *If you will accept My gift, you will.*

CHAPTER TWENTY EIGHT

Jed felt lighter than air. As he looked around him, he realized that his surroundings looked somehow familiar. His concentration was interrupted by the sudden appearance of a wagon on the road below him. He felt the urge to see the occupants of the wagon closer.

As he thought this, he felt himself moving. Being able to simply think something and have it happen gave him a heady feeling. He floated and swam his way down to the wagon. On the wagon seat sat a man and his wife. The wagon bed was loaded with supplies and children. He tried to count the children. Unless they had moved and gotten counted twice, he counted five children. Everybody looked very happy as they neared the farmhouse.

He watched as the man stopped the horses, climbed down from the wagon, and helped his wife down. The children scrambled out of the wagon bed and started unloading the supplies. He couldn't hear what was said, but from the happy looks and the laughter, he could tell that this was a happy family.

The man turned around to look back the way they had come and he thought he recognized him. His red hair and beard, his broad, muscular shoulders, quick fiery eyes. They all seemed so familiar to him. He pondered the thought, not noticing what went on below.

When he next looked, he noticed that a few years had passed. The family had a new baby and they were all very happy. But he could tell that something was not quite right.

He watched the father as he went through the motions of life on a farm. Everything seemed normal. The chores were mundane, but necessary. The man loved his family and doted on his wife. He spent plenty of time with his children and the boys were great helps on his farm. But he always seemed to be searching for an ever-elusive something.

The man was happy, but also discontented. He knew he had something missing in his life, but he could not figure out what.

The dreamer was sad for the man. He wished there was some way he could help. While thinking about this, the scene below him suddenly changed.

He was in a small room. The man below him was much older and very sick. He could tell the man would die very soon. As he watched, it became *obvious that the man was still missing something in his life. What was it? Why could he not find it?*

Another man entered the room. He could tell that this new man was a preacher. His preacher's collar stood out like a patch of snow in July. When the man saw the preacher, he became agitated and the doctor ordered the preacher to leave. The dreamer saw the preacher step outside the room and begin praying. The man calmed down, but refused to let the preacher talk to him.

He realized then that what the man needed was what the preacher had: God.

Jed woke up in a cold sweat and sat up so fast his head spun. He closed his eyes, willing the room to stand still. *Why did I just wake up?* He eased himself back into a sleeping position. He fell asleep again before he could remember what he had dreamed about.

He was floating again. He looked down at the earth and saw woods, grass, a dirt road leading somewhere, a bubbling stream heading down the hill or mountain. He narrowed his eyes in confusion. Was he supposed to see something else?

Movement to his right caught his eye. A cloud of dust. Something flashed in the sunlight. As it came closer to his view, he saw a stagecoach rolling down the road at top speed. Sunlight glinted off something directly below him. He floated closer to it and saw a man lying in wait for something. His eyes were trained down the road.

The dreamer's heart stopped. This man was about to rob the stagecoach. Didn't he know that was...

A gunshot interrupted his thought. The dreamer jerked his vision to the stage and saw the shotgun guard roll off the stage. Another gun was fired and the driver rolled off on the other side. Two men spurred their horses to intercept the racing stage. The dreamer watched as the men caught the strays and stopped the stagecoach.

The man who had shot down the guard and driver stepped out into the sunlight. It was the red-headed man again. But this time, he was with three men on an outlaw trail.

Time sped ahead. He saw the man riding with two new men. They were headed to a ranch. They broke through a fence and cut some horses out from the herd. Just as they were about to drive the horses through the fence, a young man stood up and said something. He was joined by more men. The three rustlers were handcuffed and put into a wagon.

The dreamer floated along, watching as the young sheriff put the three men in jail. Two days later, only the man was left in the jail, waiting for his trial. The dreamer could feel the man's depression and misery.

He watched as the sheriff seemed to be trying to explain something to him. The man mentally blocked his ears from hearing the encouragement and help that he was offered.

The scene changed again. This time a young woman was talking to the man. The man listened, but refused to act on what he heard.

As the days passed after the young woman left the second time, the despair and misery began to leave the man.

The dreamer was transported to another place. He saw the young woman on her knees, hands folded and head bowed. Her lips moved. The dreamer knew that her prayers were for the man. The dreamer watched as she prayed many times each day.

The scenes flickered back and forth. First he saw the young woman praying, then the man's despair slowly lifting. The young woman came into view again. The man in the cell started smiling a little. The young woman prayed by a creek. The man knelt beside his cot, hands clasped, heart crying out.

The dreamer watched as the chains around the man's heart and mind loosened and fell off and the *man started to weep. The dreamer could feel his joy. The man was free!*

It was still dark in the cell when Jed's eyes opened. He lay still for a few minutes before his brain began to register anything. His eyes stared blankly at the darkness above him. As the two dreams began to come back to him, his mind began racing.

In a daze, Jed sat up, blinking his eyes. As he recalled the dream, he suddenly recognized who the man had been. His body tensed and his breath came in short gasps. *He* had been both the man and the dreamer.

Thoughts came as fast as a runaway train. Jed's heart raced nearly as fast and his breathing became labored. "God, what do You want me to do? What does this mean?"

As soon as the words came out of his mouth, Jed's heart slowed down and his breathing became easier. The runaway train that was his thought process came to a sudden stop.

The voice that had spoken to him just a few days before spoke again, *Follow Me. Be born again.*

"Born again?" Jed's eyebrows crinkled. "What does that mean?"

Read your Bible.

Light had begun filtering into the room and there was now just enough light to read. "Okay, God, I'm ready to read, but what do I read?"

Elizabeth's words came back to him. "Read John three if you feel like reading something."

The urgency Jed felt caused him to search for the book of John and chapter three. Once he found the book, his eyes started to devour the page.

CHAPTER TWENTY NINE

"Joshua?" Micah said.

"Hmm?" Joshua continued to scribble on the paper as Micah spoke, his concentration taken up by the letter.

"Did you notice anything different about Jed today?"

Joshua's head went up and his eyes squinted at Micah. "No," he said, "I don't think so. Why?"

"I'm not sure. He just seems different today."

"Different how?"

Micah pursed his lips. "I don't know. I can't quite place my finger on it."

Joshua shrugged. "I'll pay attention next time I go in to see him."

After he finished the letter, Joshua opened the door to the jail. He looked in and saw Jed sitting on his cot reading the Bible. It looked almost as if he hadn't moved in quite some time. *What does this mean, God? Is Jed finally thinking seriously about You?* Joshua's feet started moving forward, stopping when they reached the bars to Jed's cell.

"Mornin', Jed," Joshua said.

Jed's head came up as he finished reading the sentence. He had a slight smile on his face. "Mornin', Sheriff. How are you today?"

Joshua's eyes went wide and he took a step backwards. "What?"

Jed chuckled. "I just asked how you were today."

"You've never asked that before—"

Jed held up a hand and his face sobered. "I know. I aim to change that." Jed eased off the cot. "And before you ask, I'll just go ahead and tell you." His grin grew until it reached both ears. "I became a Christian this morning."

Joshua stared at the man behind the bars. "You did?"

Jed was obviously amused by Joshua's shock. "Didn't think I could do it, did you?"

Joshua shook his head. "No, I knew you could do it, I just...I don't know. I guess I thought you might wait until the night before you were hung, not two days before your trial even begins."

Jed was thoughtful and nodded. "I'm a bit surprised, too." He paused and hesitated. "Could you get Ruth and Elizabeth here? I'd like to tell them."

Joshua grinned. "Can I sit in on it, too?"

Jed nodded.

"I'll send for them. They'll be thrilled."

It was midmorning when two very curious young women stepped into the sheriff's office.

"What is this all about, Joshua?" Ruth asked.

"Jed wants to talk to the three of us." Joshua failed in his attempt to hide the grin spreading across his face.

Elizabeth cocked an eyebrow. "Well? What are we waiting for?"

Joshua laughed as he led the way to Jed's cell. He already had three chairs set up and waiting for them. When they were all sitting down, Jed sat on the edge of his cot.

"I already told Joshua, but my guess is that he didn't tell you." Seeing the blank stares Ruth and Elizabeth gave him, Jed continued, a grin playing with his mouth. "I accepted Christ this morning."

Elizabeth squealed in delight. "That's wonderful!"

Ruth smiled. "Welcome to the family, Jed."

Jed nodded his acknowledgment.

"How—" Elizabeth began.

"That's why you're here," Jed interrupted. "I thought you all would like to hear how and I didn't feel like saying it three separate times." He licked his lips.

"Last night, I had two dreams. Both were about me. One was me as if I had not been an outlaw. I had a loving family, but something always seemed to be missing from my life. As I lay dying in my dream, a preacher tried to come in, but I chased him away. I died without ever knowing about God's love.

"In the second dream, I dreamed about one of the stagecoach robberies I did, and then of Joshua catching us after rustling his pa's horses. I saw myself sitting in this cell, depressed and miserable. Then I saw Elizabeth praying for me. As she prayed for me, I saw myself getting less and less depressed. I almost seemed joyful at times.

"Then, as I watched, I saw myself kneel beside my bed and pray. I saw the chains fall away from my heart and mind and knew I was free."

Jed took a deep breath and looked up at them. "This morning, when I woke up, I prayed for the first time ever. I asked God what I was supposed to do. He told me to be born again. I had no idea what that meant, but then I heard Elizabeth's voice tell me to read John chapter three."

Elizabeth smiled. "I knew you would like that chapter."

Jed chuckled. "I did. I don't understand it all, but it definitely helped. After I read that chapter, I knelt beside my cot and asked God to make me be born again. And He did."

"Hallelujah!" Joshua said.

"Praise the Lord!" Ruth echoed.

Elizabeth's eyes were closed and her mouth moved in a silent prayer of thanks.

They all spent a few minutes in quiet prayer. Joshua finished first. "I would love to stay here, but I have a job to do."

Ruth's eyes went wide. "Elizabeth and I left our bread in the oven. We need to get back before it burns."

Elizabeth laughed. "If it does, we will just say that it was burned for a good reason."

All four of them laughed and said their goodbyes.

Two days later, Joshua sat at his desk deep in thought. The trial had just finished and Jed was back in the cell. He had been convicted of multiple stagecoach robberies and rustling hundreds of cattle and horses. The judge sentenced him to hang to the death the next morning.

Joshua's eyes traveled to the door. He thought he heard voices outside. Yes, there they were again. The door opened.

"Son? Are you in here?"

"Pa!" Joshua jumped out of his chair. "What are you doing here? I thought you headed home."

Joshua struck a match and lit a lantern. In the doorway stood his pa and ma, Ruth, Elizabeth, and Edward Harris.

"We were," Mr. Brookings replied. "Until Ruth came up with the brilliant idea of spending the night with Jed, praying and singing hymns."

Edward cleared his throat. "I doubt he'll sleep a wink tonight anyway."

Tears sprang to Joshua's eyes. "You hear that, Jed?" he called behind him.

A choked voice answered, "I heard."

Joshua's knuckles turned white as he gripped the lantern and led the group down the hall to Jed's cell. Joshua handed the lantern to his pa and looked Jed straight in the eyes. "Jed, I'd like to have the whole group of us together, without bars between us, but the only way to do that is to leave the bars unlocked. Do you promise not to try to get away? We'll all be between you and the door."

Jed kept his gaze steady. "I promise not to run off on you." He reached out a hand. Joshua took it in his and they shook hands.

Joshua took the key out of his pocket and unlocked the bars. Mr. Brookings and Mr. Harris were the first to enter the cell. Mrs. Brookings followed with Joshua close behind. Ruth and Elizabeth both hung back. The cell was crowded with all of them inside, but it wasn't too uncomfortable.

Daniel Brookings looked at his daughter. "You were the one with this idea. Would you like to get us started?"

Ruth blushed. "I guess I can." She was silent for a moment, her head bowed. The silence calmed and comforted them all. Ruth began in a quiet voice. So quiet that at first she could barely be heard as she began to sing. Then her voice grew stronger.

> *"A mighty fortress is our God,*
> *A bulwark never failing;*
> *Our helper he amid the flood*
> *Of mortal ills prevailing."*

Joshua smiled as he recognized the hymn and closed his eyes as he joined in the singing with his rich baritone. Daniel, Harriet, and Mr. Harris all joined in the singing. Elizabeth waited until the start of the second verse before joining in with the harmony.

> *"For still our ancient foe*
> *Doth seek to work us woe;*
> *His craft and power are great,*
> *And armed with cruel hate,*
> *On earth is not his equal.*

"Did we in our own strength confide,
Our striving would be losing,
Were not the right man on our side,
The man of God's own choosing.
Dost ask who that may be?
Christ Jesus, it is he;
Lord Sabaoth, his name,
From age to age the same,
And he must win the battle.

"And though this world, with devils
filled,
Should threaten to undo us,
We will not fear, for God hath willed
His truth to triumph through us.
The Prince of Darkness grim,
We tremble not for him;
His rage we can endure,
For lo, his doom is sure;
One little word shall fell him.

"That word above all earthly powers,
No thanks to them, abideth;
The Spirit and the gifts are ours,
Through him who with us sideth.
Let goods and kindred go,
This mortal life also;
The body they may kill;
God's truth abideth still;

318

His kingdom is forever."

"Heavenly Father," Daniel prayed, "we come before You today with conflicted hearts. We are overjoyed that Jed has joined the family of God. But we are also saddened knowing that, because of his wrong choices earlier in his life, he will not have a chance to live life to the fullest here on earth. Father, give Jed peace tonight. Keep him strong tomorrow as he faces the gallows."

Joshua listened as each of them took turns praying. They prayed mostly for Jed, but also for each other. Mr. Harris prayed for strength for Elizabeth as she watched the hanging in the morning. Mr. Brookings prayed the same for Ruth and Joshua.

When each of them had prayed at least once, Joshua started singing his favorite Psalm: Psalm 91.

He that dwelleth in the secret place of the most High shall abide under the shadow of the Almighty.

I will say of the Lord, He is my refuge and my fortress: my God; in him will I trust.

Surely he shall deliver thee from the snare of the fowler, and from the noisome pestilence.

He shall cover thee with his feathers, and under his wings shalt thou trust: his truth shall be thy shield and buckler.

Thou shalt not be afraid for the terror by night; nor for the arrow that flieth by day;

Nor for the pestilence that walketh in darkness; nor for the destruction that wasteth at noonday.

A thousand shall fall at thy side, and ten thousand at thy right hand; but it shall not come nigh thee—

Joshua watched Jed as they sang. Jed's face still looked hardened from his years as an outlaw, but it also seemed somehow softer.

When the singing was finished, Jed opened his eyes. "Can you teach me the first hymn you sang?"

Ruth grinned. "We'd be happy to."

It took them nearly the rest of the night, but Jed finally had "A Mighty Fortress" memorized. A sense of peace flooded over Joshua and as he looked at Jed and their eyes met, he knew the same feeling had come over him.

The sun broke over the hills and light flooded into the small cell.

Jed looked around at the people surrounding him. "Thank you." His voice broke and he struggled to take a breath. "Last night was the best night of my life."

Joshua looked at his pocket watch. "Four hours yet. We'll leave you alone for that time. Is there anything specific you would like for breakfast?"

Jed shook his head, then changed his mind. "Actually yes, I would rather not have anything for breakfast." He smiled grimly. "I don't really see the point of it when I'll be feasting in just a few more hours."

A couple of nervous laughs were heard throughout the group. "You have a point there," Mr. Harris said as he put a hand on his daughter's shoulder. "Let's go find someplace to get some rest for a couple hours and then meet at the café for breakfast. I'm buying."

Joshua was the last to leave the cell. He turned and locked the door. "God bless you, Jed," he said quietly as he turned to leave.

"Thank you for everything, Joshua. I know that none of this was easy for you."

Joshua nodded. "No, it wasn't. But, it was all worth it. Seeing you here as a brother in Christ. Knowing I'll see you again in heaven. That makes it all worth it."

Jed swallowed hard and nodded.

"I'll leave you alone with God now. If you need anything, I'll be in my office. I'll leave the door open."

"Thank you."

It's the least I can do, Joshua thought to himself as he left Jed alone. *It's the least I can do.*

CHAPTER THIRTY

Elizabeth stood at the edge of the crowd next to Ruth. They clutched each other in a tight embrace, gathering strength each from the other. Elizabeth felt Ruth trembling. "It'll be all right," Elizabeth whispered. "It'll be all right. Jed is going to a better place now. He'll be happier there."

Ruth shuddered. "I know that, but I wish...I know he deserves what he is getting, but I still wish he could have somehow been pardoned." Ruth turned to face Elizabeth. "He's a new man now. He deserves to have a new life."

"He does have a new life. It was only for a few days, but he said it was the happiest three days of his life."

Ruth smiled. "Did you know he even wrote to his family?"

Elizabeth looked at her in surprise. "No, I didn't."

"Yes, he wrote to them asking for their forgiveness and telling them about what Jesus did for him."

Elizabeth's smile broadened. "Good for him."

The crowd suddenly hushed their talking. Ruth and Elizabeth turned and saw Joshua leading Jed to the gallows.

"God, give him Your strength and peace," Elizabeth whispered.

"Amen," Ruth said.

Elizabeth kept her eyes on Jed's face. He seemed peaceful so far. There was a flicker of fear and dread as his eyes caught sight of the gallows. *Thank You, God, for forgiving Jed and for leading him to You.*

Jed slowly climbed the ladder to the platform. The judge stood at the top waiting for him. He motioned for Jed to stand next to him. Joshua stood just behind and to the left of Jed. Judge Parker took a piece of paper and his eyeglasses out of his shirt pocket. He put the eyeglasses firmly on his nose and held the paper in front of his face.

"By the power vested in me by the Territory of Montana, I hereby sentence Jedidiah Iain Stuart to hang to death for various crimes, including, but not limited to, cattle and horse rustling, robbery, and murder." Judge Parker turned to Jed. "Do you have any last words?"

Jed nodded.

Elizabeth tried to swallow the lump forming in her throat. *God, give him the words to say.* She watched as Jed blinked his eyes and swallowed two or three times before speaking in an emotional, but firm voice.

"Most o' you don't know me as I never stepped foot in yer town. You only know 'bout me. You know that I'm the one who rustled yer cattle and horses, or that of yer neighbor or friend. You may even know that I'm the one who robbed the stagecoach that Joshua and Ruth Brookings were on and then chased 'em through the wilderness to kill them."

Jed dropped his eyes to the wooden boards holding him up off the ground. "All these things I'm now ashamed of. Four days ago, I was proud of my prowess at not bein' caught for so many years. Three days ago, my outlook on life changed because of the influence and prayers of those who knew me best. Because of those who knew my faults best, I came to learn about and to know God personally. Three days ago, I let God take control of my life."

Jed looked up and searched the crowd. His eyes met Elizabeth's from across the crowd and he gave a slight nod. A sad smile lit on his face. "I have never felt more free than the moment I surrendered my life to God's control."

Elizabeth watched as Jed turned Joshua's direction. She saw them whisper for a few seconds, then Joshua walked over to talk to the judge. Joshua's eyes were expressive as he argued his case to the judge. The judge finally relented and Joshua gave Jed a quick nod before he spoke.

"Ladies and Gentlemen, last night, my family and our guests spent the night with Jed praying and singing hymns. During that time, we taught Jed one of our favorite hymns. Judge Parker has granted Jed one final request." Joshua turned toward Jed. "You may make your request."

Jed's eyes gazed at Joshua in deep gratitude. "Would Elizabeth Harris and Ruth Brookings please come up here?"

Elizabeth looked at Ruth. Ruth's eyes were as wide as her own. Elizabeth grabbed Ruth's hand and they walked to the gallows together. Elizabeth let Ruth go up the ladder first. When Elizabeth reached the top, Joshua stood next to Ruth waiting for her.

"Jed wants to sing the first three verses of 'A Mighty Fortress' with us and then he will stop singing and go..." Joshua's voice cracked. "Then we'll sing the last verse." Joshua's voice was raw with emotion.

Elizabeth stared at him, eyes wide. "I'm not sure I can do that."

Ruth clutched Joshua's arm. "I *know* I can't do that. I won't be able to sing that last verse."

Joshua looked at them. "I know it'll be hard. It may very well be the hardest thing any of us will ever do, but it is Jed's last request." Joshua took a deep breath and closed his eyes. "God, give our voices strength and give us the courage to grant Jed this last request."

Ruth stifled a sob as Joshua hooked his elbow into hers. Elizabeth held on to Ruth's other hand and they walked to the edge of the platform to stand next to Jed.

Elizabeth closed her eyes and waited for Jed to start singing. His slightly off-key bass combined with Ruth's soprano and Joshua's baritone. Elizabeth sang the harmony in her clear alto.

Elizabeth kept her eyes closed until the end of the second verse. When she opened them, she let her eyes wander among the crowd. Not one eye that she could see was dry.

The third verse ended and Jed's voice dropped out. The singing faltered for a few notes as they all swallowed the lumps forming in their throats. Even while they sang, Elizabeth could hear Jed's boots walking toward the noose.

She kept her eyes fixed on a lone bush growing in a front yard. She knew if she closed her eyes the only thing she would see would be the hangman's knot slipping over Jed's head. *God, keep my voice strong!*

Jed's footsteps stopped. Elizabeth heard the swish of a rope falling. There was a moment's pause before the trapdoor snapped open and Elizabeth had to force herself to think only about the words as she sang the final phrase of the hymn that would usher Jed into heaven:

> *"Let goods and kindred go,*
> *This mortal life also;*
> *The body they may kill;*
> *God's truth abideth still;*
> *His kingdom is forever."*

Please share this book with a friend.

Please recommend this book.
Good books are meant to be shared. If you enjoyed this book, let a friend know about it.

Please post a review.
Reviews are important to authors and helps other customers find books and make the decision whether or not to buy them. Reviews are especially helpful to Indie authors such as myself. Please take a few minutes and leave an honest review on http://amazon.com and/or http://goodreads.com. Thank you!

Please read more in the series.
This is the first novel in the series. Go to my author page on Amazon to find more books.

PREVIEW

Keep reading for a special preview of the next book in the series by Faith Blum!

Hymns of the West #2
Be Thou My Vision

Another encouraging sermon and uplifting service over with. I sat in the pew extra long today. I seemed to be in need of a little extra quiet and peace. I knew Da and Caleb were both resenting my time spent in church lately and I dreaded going home.

The church was empty before I finally dragged myself up out of the pew and headed out the door. I walked down the steps and was nearly bowled over by two wild boys. Arms grown strong and quick from manhandling two brothers growing up, I grabbed the two boys before they had a chance to escape me.

Turning their faces toward me so I could see who the offending parties were, I was surprised to see James and John.

"What is going on here?" I demanded. "Why are you two acting like heathen wild men?"

"We didn't mean no harm, Miss Stuart. Honestly we didn't."

I screwed my eyes shut at John's grammar. "You didn't mean *any* harm. Really, John. Don't you pay attention at school? I know your ma's dead, but doesn't your da do anything to correct your grammar?" James and John both looked up at me with eyes full of...something. I wasn't sure what. Disbelief? But disbelief about what?

"Take me to yer da, boys. I'd like to have a wee bit of a talk with him."

SPECIAL THANKS

This book would have never made it to publication without all the help I received from many friends. Many thanks go to Aubrey Hansen and Perry Kirkpatrick, who took the time to answer my many questions about how to publish my book.

Garry Wright, I never would have made it this far without your constant encouragement and cheerleading. Often when I was down or unmotivated, I would receive an email from you and you would encourage me, even if you didn't know you were doing so. Thank you, Garry!

I never could have gotten this book finished this quickly without my family picking up some of the slack while I was writing, editing, and researching. Thanks Dad, Mom, Lydia, Naomi, and Seth!

Many thanks to Kelsey Bryant, Garry Wright, Jamie Fredrickson, Brian Smith, Bethany Baldwin, Resha Caner, Lou Farris, Gail Blum, Lydia Blum, Naomi Blum, and Aubrey Hansen for all your work beta reading, proofreading, and formatting. I never could have done this without you all.

And last, but certainly not least, I thank my Savior and Lord, Jesus Christ, for dying on the cross for my sins and saving me from eternal damnation in hell.

ABOUT THE AUTHOR

Faith Blum started writing at an early age. She started even before she could read! She even thought she could write better than Dr. Seuss. (The picture doesn't show it well, but there are scribblings on the page of *Green Eggs and Ham*). Now that she has grown up a little more, she knows she will probably never reach the success of Dr. Seuss, but that doesn't stop her from trying.

When she isn't writing, Faith enjoys doing many right-brained activities such as reading, crafting, writing, playing piano, and playing games with her family. One of her dreams is to visit Castle City, Montana someday to see the ghost town she chose for her characters to live in. She currently lives on a hobby farm with her family in Wisconsin.

There are many ways to connect with Faith online. All of them can be found in one convenient place: http://FaithBlum.com. On her website, you can find her on various social media sites as well as her blog.

50369067R00212

Made in the USA
San Bernardino, CA
20 June 2017